The Darkness of Magic
Book One

Tania Joanne Peterson

ISBN: 978-0-6488410-0-5 (Paperback)
         978-0-6488410-1-2 (eBook)

 A catalogue record for this book is available from the National Library of Australia

Editor: Adriane Hesselbein from Upwork.com
Cover Design: Ocean Reeve Publishing
Design and Typeset: Ocean Reeve Publishing
Printed in Australia by Ocean Reeve Publishing

Self-Published by Tania Joanne Peterson, PO Box 470, Neutral Bay Junction 2089 NSW.
Assisted by Genesis Publishing
A self-publishing imprint of Ocean Reeve Publishing

This book is dedicated to my father, Desmond Darnley (known as 'Danny') Peterson. Love you, Dad!

Chapter One

Queen's Chamber, Barakten
Evening
Yella Speaks

I still don't know how I put myself under such a deep trance when I was so damn terrified.

But let me explain my story from the beginning.

"Tell us exactly what happened to Queen Elsbeth," a man with dark hair and eyes said roughly, "and we won't execute you. We won't donate your dead body to the vultures outside these walls. Don't worry, you shouldn't have any trouble. You're a psychic, aren't you?" he sneered.

I was standing in a meeting room inside the palace walls, surrounded by eight very stern-looking royal court officials. My heart beat savagely in my chest, but I answered as calmly as I could. "The best way for me to do that is to surround myself in Her Majesty's energy," I explained. "By that, I mean touching objects that she most frequently touches."

They stared at me with confused looks on their faces. I decided to elaborate. "The more we touch something, the more we leave what I call an 'energy imprint' on that object that can be psychically read and interpreted by a sensitive like me. I think her bedroom's a good place to start, as she may have disappeared at night. Can I lie in her bed?"

Surprisingly they allowed it, so we were soon walking down a long corridor and before I knew it, I was lying in the massive bed of her Royal Highness Queen Elsbeth II with eight men staring at me. They must've thought I was mad, squirming and moving around as if I was making love to the sheets. I didn't care. They didn't know anything about me or my psychic work or how I did my psychic work; appearing odd was the least of my worries.

They also didn't know how determined I was to get the answers. I genuinely loved the Queen and besides, as a twenty-three-year-old man, I was far too young to die.

I first fell in love with Queen Elsbeth at a public event when I was sixteen years old. She was travelling in a carriage with her parents and looked about the same age as me. When our eyes met briefly and locked, it was as if time had stood still, then punched me in the face. We'd shared many lifetimes together, and I'd loved her in those lifetimes; sometimes even more than I loved myself. We'd been together once and would be again, I knew it. I just didn't know *how* I knew it.

She'd never been what you would call a 'popular' Queen. The Baraktenian citizens were happy to dismiss her as a villain because that's what they were like; constant slaves to gossip and what they'd been told. Slaves to what they could only see, hear or touch. It was so typical of those gossipy, empty-headed surface dwellers to think like that. But below the surface another world can flourish, a world that can escape the eyes. A world of stories – stories possibly not yet even told. What lies beneath, I eternally wonder; truth or lies? Or a confusing mishmash of both?

Who or what was the real enemy to the Baraktenian people? Queen Elsbeth, or their own blind acceptance of someone else's truth? Could there be other enemies hidden in the shadows, and if so, would they strike again? Enemies don't have to be seen to strike.

Elsbeth had such an enemy. She disappeared without a trace a week ago, with only an opened window in her bedchamber for evidence, and no-one heard or saw a thing. Not even the guards. That's why they consulted me, a well-known psychic in Barakten, to help find her.

A very scared psychic at that point in time as eight men stared at me, surrounding the bed I was lying in, demanding answers. Illuminated by the tall, white candles that gently lit the room, they looked more like ghosts ready to take me to the afterlife.

I prayed, set my intention and psychically protected myself with white light. Then I meditated by repeating a sacred mantra and concentrated, and soon a sinking feeling overcame me as my body began to relax and my mind began to quieten.

I don't remember the exact point that I dropped into a deep trance; I just remember feeling suddenly there, blissfully peaceful and still, as if floating happily underwater in a deep well but I could still see and breathe easily. All fear, all ego and all sense of time and place had gone, replaced by nothing but a wonderful sense of mindlessness; of ceased thought, where I became one with my surroundings instead of separate from them, merging into a single state of consciousness.

Mercifully, the vision came.

"I see them," I said.

"What?" asked a voice, "What do you see?"

Although he stood very close, he sounded far away, as if he was calling me. I continued on with my eyes closed. "Two men climb through her window. One's much taller than the other. They reach her sleeping in bed. The tall one puts his hand over her

3

mouth and carries her struggling through the window outside. Two winged animals are waiting there, with torsos the size of a horse. I've not seen the creatures before. They're strange. They're leathery, four-legged and greyish in colour, with lizard-like heads. They've long tails and sharp teeth and long forked tongues…"

"Studdgartas," a voice said to grunts of agreement.

"The tall one's rough," I said, flinching because I felt the strength of his grip. "He jumps onto the animal's back with her in his arms. They're flying. The other one follows, jumping onto the other animal and trailing. The hands of the tall one hurt," I gasped. "They're digging into her so hard…nearly crushing her mouth…but she can't plead with him to let her go—"

My words cut off, as did my air. "Breathe!" I shouted, suddenly thrashing around the bed in a panic. "I…can't…breathe!"

Fortunately the awful sensation didn't last long, but I gasped and panted loudly as I recovered.

"Where's she going?" a voice demanded roughly.

"Sarakonia," I replied, still panting heavily.

"Are you certain?" another man asked. His tone was threatening.

"I know it," I managed in between breaths. "I just don't know how I know it. They're taking her to a prison."

This announcement didn't please the royal court officials. The Baraktenian Desert lay between the countries of Barakten and Sarakonia, a territory well known for its treachery – it had a long and colorful history of killing many who dared to cross it. The vast array of voices continued talking above me as my breathing calmed down and my mood changed – I started to peacefully drift and sway.

"Sarakonia? We can't send our soldiers there. It's too dangerous; too many lives would be lost, and that's far too costly."

"Surely we can afford to send around thirty soldiers?" a voice reasoned. "Don't forget, these are highly trained men and women who know the ways of the desert. We could logically expect to lose only around five in the journey; ten at most."

"But can we believe–"

"I'll find you Elsbeth," I interrupted dreamily. "I promise." A vision of the Queen had just come into my mind, all blue-eyed and lovely, and I smiled.

There were strong murmurings of disapproval around the room.

"Address Her Majesty by her proper name and title, you insolent bastard," an official barked.

"We know each other well," I explained. "Through many lifetimes."

"Why take her to Sarakonia?" a voice demanded.

There was nothing to say to that, so I just floated around in my peaceful abyss while they talked. And talked. And talked. And talked…

"This is horseshit. How about I beat more information out of him?" a voice suggested.

"You'll do no such thing," came a reply.

"It'll give us what we want," the voice argued.

"It'll stop the visions in his head. His visions are all we've got, so you can back off with your theories *and* your fist!" There were sounds of scuffling and curses.

"How can he be trusted? For all we know, this might be a grand theatrical performance, put on to save his neck."

"I agree," another voice said. "We've got to be certain of this. If we send soldiers to Sarakonia, lives will be lost because of him, we can be sure of that."

Different voices came into the discussion.

"This is ridiculous. We're supposed to get the *facts*, not someone panting and blabbering on."

"We're aware of that, but Her Majesty's vanished and we've got nothing else to go by."

"So we go by *him*?"

"He's the best psychic in the country. He's located countless missing, both alive and dead – that's why he's here, isn't it? Because he's a genius?"

"He's no genius, he's *odd*."

"He's a strange one, I'll give you that, but I believe in what he says."

"I agree," another voice interjected. "His record's impeccable."

"I don't know if I'm terribly comfortable with sending soldiers to their death over a vision," a voice said tersely.

"But what if it's correct? What if Her Majesty dies because we didn't send our soldiers to Sarakonia? Are we more concerned for the lives of a small handful of disposable soldiers over that of our own Queen?"

"We've got to make a decision."

There was a long pause, where I could almost feel the burn of collective eyes resting on me, then someone said, "Yella Fella. Do you have anything more to say to us?"

They waited patiently for several minutes for me to answer, but I said nothing. They babbled on for a few more minutes, till one of them came up close, clapping a firm hand on my shoulder. I jolted slightly with the impact.

"It seems this is the end of your trance." The voice was deep and authoritative.

"Yes," I whispered. "It's over now."

"This has been a major disappointment to us," the same voice continued. "We expected that a man with your supposed 'psychic' abilities would provide us with more information than that. You've given us almost nothing to work on. We needed important facts in this matter, such as names. More specific locations. Motives. You've failed in your duty to Her Majesty, and I'm afraid the penalty for that is execution." He paused meaningfully. "Do you understand what I've just said?"

They meant to kill me. I mentally clawed closer to the surface of waking consciousness, away from the abyss of trance, so I could hopefully start making more sense, but I felt a heaviness pulling me back. "Give me another chance," I protested drowsily. "Just two more days. I'll give you more information then, I swear."

"Two more days," he repeated thoughtfully. There was another long, almost unbearable pause. "We will discuss it."

"Why are we wasting our time? Just execute the lying piece of shit," another voice said.

The weight of their words fully registered in my brain, and I tried again to beg and plead for my life by saying something. Anything! But this time my tongue wouldn't co-operate with me; instead, it made sounds like the senseless babble of an infant, and the only other sound after that was the heaviness of a slammed door before I sank into sleep.

❦

Baraktenian Desert

A thirty-five-year-old spice merchant named Jet Black sat cross-legged, staring into the crackling flames of a campfire as he peacefully sipped a cup of tea. He was strikingly handsome to look at, with penetrating dark-brown eyes, shoulder-length black hair, olive skin, and a strong, stocky body. A tattoo of a dragon adorned his right breast and arm, an image symbolizing great wisdom and courage; qualities he always thought were essential for survival in the desert. Especially the Baraktenian Desert.

Suddenly there was a distinct rustling noise in the darkness coming from the bushes nearby. Curious, he cocked his head to the side, carefully laying his cup of tea on the ground as he slowly stood up to investigate. Creeping towards the bushes, he grabbed a thick, broken-off tree branch from the ground on his way. He peered into the darkness and saw nothing. Whatever it was could have crawled into—

"Get him!"

At the speed of light two desert pigs charged him and he soon found himself desperately trying to beat them off with all his strength. One viciously tugged at a trouser leg, while the second pig tugged at the other. Grunting and gritting his teeth, he kept on solidly beating their backs with the branch until they finally decided to let go, fleeing back to the cover of darkness.

Trembling and panting heavily, he held the branch at the ready in front of him in anticipation of another attack when he suddenly heard a male voice coming from behind.

"I say sir."

He turned to the direction of the voice and saw an ordinary-sized desert pig only meters away, illuminated by the campfire. Confused, he quickly looked around to see where the voice was coming from.

"No need to look, sir. It's my voice you heard," the pig said.

"You can talk," he exclaimed, stating the obvious.

"And read and write also," the pig added matter-of-factly.

"But that – that's impossible," Jet stammered, hardly believing what his eyes and ears were telling him.

"Actually, I used to be a librarian in Barakten before Her Majesty Queen Elsbeth turned me into a pig. I miss my books and study," he said longingly. "By the way, do you know I also happen to be partially blind?"

"No," Jet replied, feeling weird about conversing with a pig.

"Blind in one eye since the day I was born, and the other one's not so good either. But I'm being rude – I must introduce myself. The name's Arvid. And you are?"

"Jet," he stammered. "Jet Black."

"Pleased to meet you Mister Black," the pig said. "I see you've already met my two comrades. I hope you excuse their rudeness. They just wanted to tear your limbs off, eat you and then steal your food and water supplies, that's all. Instinct, you see. Nothing personal. I tend to be a more refined pig. I thought you might feed and water us if I asked you politely and then I thought afterwards we might engage in some intelligent conversation. Do you like to read?" he asked eagerly. "And if so, do you have a favorite author?"

Jet looked to the bushes where he thought the other pigs might still be hiding. "*They're* your comrades? The animals that just tried to rip me to pieces?"

The pig chuckled. "Believe me sir, if you're hungry enough, you'll eat anything. And you look juicy enough." His small, piggy eyes seemed to glint evilly in the fire light, sending a sickening shiver up Jet's spine.

"Stick to desert mice, like you're *supposed* to do, and get away from me!" Jet yelled in disgust, reaching for the biggest rock he could find and hurling it at him.

But the pig was too quick and agile for him and dodged the rock just in time, running to the protective cover of darkness again. "I'm still here!" he taunted from behind the bushes. "And you're a rotten shot," he added.

"I'll have another go then!" Jet shouted, hurling another rock at him. "You ugly piece of shit!"

"Be careful who you insult, you rude, uneducated and unrefined prick!" Arvid shot back.

"Yeah! We got teeth ya know, and we're not afraid to use 'em!" another voice yelled.

"Stay awake all night tonight, because as soon as your eyes close, we'll tear you apart and I'm personally going to enjoy every single damn second of it," Arvid spat nastily.

Jet reacted by picking the branch up again and, holding it tightly, slowly and cautiously moved as close as he possibly could to the fire. He was panting a little from fear but forced himself to calm down and think. He wouldn't be able to pack up his tent and leave, or even quickly try to search for the knife he kept in there – it was far too risky with three savage talking desert pigs (who moved like lightning and couldn't be seen very well) waiting to pounce on him.

But standing upright all night with a stick in his hands was equally as risky. All it'd take was one single moment of inattention, one closed eye, and they'd charge at him and tear him to pieces. Eat him alive as they promised they would. And now it'd definitely be three pigs attacking him, instead of two. All of which meant that the only remaining logical solution to this very dangerous predicament was…

"Arvid!" he yelled. "Arvid!"

He waited for a response. There wasn't one.

"Please forgive my rudeness. It's not every day I meet a talking animal and you've taken me by surprise. Come. Dine with me. You and your friends. There's enough food and water for all of us and there's certainly no need for such uncivilized fighting. Please."

Silence.

"I want to talk with you," he pleaded. "I have fine wine. Come and drink with me – share your stories. I want to hear your stories, Arvid." He paused. "Arvid?"

Silence again.

He thought furiously. This was bullshit. He was getting nowhere with them, dammit. He needed their trust and friendship, his life depended on it. After further deliberation, he decided to pull out the most powerful drawing card he had – his God-given psychic ability – and tuned his mind into those of the pigs.

"Arvid," he said loudly, "you've just told me you were human once and I'm seeing it now in my mind's eye. I see all of you: long-haired, bearded men in leather and cloth."

He heard a distinct rustling in the bushes and was encouraged by it.

He continued talking rapidly, as he worked best when he talked at speed. "You're all Baraktenians, aren't you? I feel it. I feel your lives have been stolen from you – wives and children taken, never to be seen again. One of you had a lover, kept secret from others. Your hearts are bitter and vengeful, and I can definitely lend a sympathetic ear to that, as I happen to hold another career as a counselor back home. I feel one of you used to work with wood. A carpenter maybe? I hear hammering and–"

Voices in the distance loudly interrupted.

"Unbelievable. How did he know this shit?"

"Yeah yeah yeah, it's impressive, but something's off. He doesn't *smell* right."

"What are you saying?"

"I'm saying we should *eat* him, as opposed to *listening* to him."

"That's not very civilized, Amus."

"Who gives a shit? We're animals anyway, and I don't trust him."

"I've waited too long for fine food, fine wine and intelligent conversation." It was Arvid's voice again. "Come on you lot – this sounds exciting. Let's summon our human side and be civilized for once."

Jet saw three pigs trotting out of the bushes to his right and smiled broadly as he turned to them, quickly tossing away the branch in his hands.

"Right, who are you?" Arvid demanded. "Do you come from Barakten?"

"No, Sarakonia."

"Have you always been psychic?" Arvid asked. "Or did you get hit on the head and gain special powers or something?"

"The gift's been with me since the age of five. No accidents needed."

"How interesting," Arvid said, clearly impressed. "I've never met a psychic before."

"Well it's commonplace where I come from. Almost a quarter of the citizens are either psychic, or keen practitioners of magic." He cocked his head to the side as he considered them all thoughtfully. "Who turned you into pigs, by the way?"

"Queen Elsbeth had a court sorcerer–" Arvid began.

"Say no more," Jet nodded. "How long's it been now?"

"Too long," another pig butted in.

"Really?"

"How would *you* like hanging around two ugly, smelly bastards all day?"

"Kiss my ass," the pig next to him said.

"I don't have to – I *smell* it all the time," he retorted.

"Fuck off!"

Jet smiled. "You should come with me to my homeland of Sarakonia. My bike's large enough to accommodate everyone.

I sense you'll find happiness there. Believe me, to them there's no such thing as strangeness or oddities. You'll fit in there, be embraced as their own, and most importantly, they also have baths." He gave a mischievous wink.

"Now *that* sounds like poetry to the ears," Arvid said approvingly.

"Good," Jet nodded. "*Now* can we sit together and talk? Especially when there's clearly so much to discuss? I travel alone as you can see, and could do with the company."

"Can you tell us our future?" one of the pigs asked.

"Of course," he replied. "It'd be an honor, as I see only good things ahead."

"Forget about our future," another pig said. "I wanna get drunk."

"Like I said, I'd be more than happy to share my wine with you. I'll get some bowls."

The three pigs looked at each other, then grunted and nodded, as if they were all communicating in some sort of secret code. Then they shape-shifted into men before his very eyes, in the same form he'd seen in his mind's eye. Jet wasn't expecting it and in complete shock, took an instinctive step backwards.

"Save the bowl, I prefer a cup." Arvid smiled. "As I said, I'm the refined one."

He was a plain man of thin build and looked to be in his mid-thirties. He was blue-eyed, and his fine dark-blonde hair was tamed into a long, neat braid that travelled halfway down his back. He wore small, round glasses and had a silver hooped earring in one ear.

Jet stared at them, momentarily losing his power of speech.

"It seems we possess more talents than you imagined possible," Arvid said with a friendly smile.

"It seems you do," Jet agreed, raising his eyebrows. "Yet we all have an animal inside us, don't we, at one time or another?"

"Well when's yours coming out then?" Arvid asked playfully.

Jet smiled. "Maybe after dinner and a few drinks?"

Everyone laughed.

"By the way, you were spot on with your psychic sense," Arvid said. "We're all Baraktenians."

"But catch us on a bad day and we're a bunch of no-good, rotten pigs," his friend wisecracked. He was a tall, skinny, bony man, with a ruddy complexion, missing front tooth, and a long, crooked nose. The ugly one of the three, Jet decided. He too was covered in tattoos, but he was much older looking than his friends – possibly mid-forties, with long, dirty brown hair tamed roughly into a tight, greasy bun.

"Allow me to introduce my comrades," Arvid said. "This is Amus."

The third one nodded coolly, a stocky, broad-shouldered, heavily tattooed man with large brown eyes and thick, long black hair tied back in a ponytail. Late-twenties, Jet guessed, and sur-ly-looking.

"And this is Rox," Arvid said, indicating the ugly one with his head. "He misses his booze."

"That's not all I miss," Rox corrected. "Don't forget me lovely wife and children. I just happened to mention the booze first."

"Rox was a carpenter by trade in Barakten and Amus was a baker," Arvid explained. "Both left behind wives and children as you said. I was the one with the secret lover."

"How come you never told us about your secret lover?" Rox asked.

"If I told you, it'd no longer be a secret then, would it?" he answered, rolling his eyes.

"Um, okay."

"Excuse me while I get the wine and food," Jet said, getting down to business. "Sit down and make yourselves comfortable – this won't take long."

Arvid and Rox did as they were told while he busied himself inside the tent, but Amus refused, announcing he was taking a walk.

"Amus," Arvid scolded, "I know it's been a long time since we've seen another person, but this is bordering on paranoia."

"Come on man, what can he do to us?" Rox reasoned. "It's three against one and besides, he's not a soldier or anything, is he? He's just a crummy two-bit pissy merchant – unarmed and with food and wine, no less."

"Tell someone who gives a shit," Amus said stubbornly. "Unlike you lot, I listen to my gut, and it's tellin' me something's wrong. You should try it some time."

"How long has it been since we've had decent human food, eh?" Arvid said. "We've been eating mice and ants and tarantulas. Mice and ants and tarantulas for God's sake. I don't understand you. Something better gets literally *thrown* in your face and you don't want it."

Something tipped the balance in Amus and he exploded. "I've been given this fuckin' dirty pig nose for a reason and I'm using it! And I'm telling you, he doesn't smell right! Something's off! And to answer your question, yeah, I do want something better for myself! I want my old life in Barakten back!" He was shouting and pacing angrily. "I wanna see my wife again! I wanna look into those pretty blue eyes! I wanna see my little babies grow up! I wanna bake like I used to and live like a normal son-of-a-bitch again! But you think that's gonna happen? Huh?"

"Stop it!" Arvid demanded. "You're not the only one! Rox and I have also lost, remember? Let's not give in to our grief–"

"Is that supposed to make me feel any better?" Amus barked. "Because it's not fucking working!"

"Well in case you haven't noticed, fucking hysteria doesn't work that well either!" Arvid shot back.

There was a brief pause as the two men, breathing heavily, glared at each other.

"Dammit Amus," Arvid said, tapping the side of his head. "Think. This man can help us. Lead us to a brand-new country. Give us a chance to start over, and–"

"Sorry. Still not working. And he doesn't smell any better either."

"Getting away from both this awful desert and you lot. Sounds like a good deal to me," Rox mused. "In fact, it sounds like friggin' heaven."

"The last thing I need is going even further from the wife and kids," Amus said, voice straining with emotion.

Now it was Arvid's turn to raise his voice. "Be a man and face the facts, you stubborn asshole!" he said. "We're all fucked, and this might be our only hope. Do you understand? Our one and only chance of getting un-fucked. What are you expecting, anyway?" he asked as he cocked his head to the side. "Huh? For your wife and kids to somehow magically appear? Maybe spring out of a sand dune somewhere? Carrying a nice tray of puffy cream cakes?"

And then, despite fiercely trying to fight them off, he felt the tears come, gracefully flowing down his cheeks like a slow-moving river. "For fuck's sake," he said as he shakily wiped them away. "Will you just…let go? Get on with things? Like Rox and I do every fucking day of our fucking miserable lives?"

Amus always did this crap, Arvid thought bitterly. Go on and on with the emotional baggage. It often ended with everyone in tears, and he was getting fed up with it. He was worse than a woman, dammit.

"Fuck," Rox said, sniveling and watery-eyed. "This is so depressing. Where's that man's booze?"

"You two do what you like, who gives a shit. I'm not giving up," Amus said.

"We gotta move forward, don't we?" Rox reasoned. "Ya know, soldier on and all that?"

"Go fuck yourselves!" With that final verbal insult Amus dived into the sand, turning into a pig a split second before entering the earth.

"Amus, please! Come back!" Arvid pleaded, diving in after him. He too turned into a pig a split second before entering the ground.

Hearing the ruckus, Jet cautiously emerged from the tent. "Uh, everything all right here gentlemen?"

"No, it's not alright," Rox said. "I'm stuck in a desert with two crazy people and I need a drink."

"There'll be plenty of opportunities for that after dinner," Jet pointed out.

"Aww come on," Rox protested. "I'll pay ya."

"With what?"

"Whaddaya want? An arm? A leg? A testicle?"

Arvid emerged from the ground up to his waist in human form. "I'm sorry, Jet. We're all damaged goods," he said, sighing as he heaved himself up from the earth. "But believe you me, I'm still more than up for a conversation."

Jet neatly laid the food and water out before them and they ate ravenously, eagerly stuffing their mouths with wonderful, proper human food. A short time later, the men became much more relaxed and conversational as they drank wine together.

They told him their story: several months ago, Queen Elsbeth II had a new policy – a new vision for Barakten. She wanted 'unblemished' citizens, and that meant getting rid of the physically and mentally disabled from its population. Five weeks ago, her policy was implemented, and hundreds of 'blemished' citizens were banished, sent away by force to live in the Baraktenian Desert.

There was an ugly riot, as some decided to put up a fight. To solve that problem, she had a sorcerer turn all the banished ones into pigs, immediately making them a lot more transportable. They were captured in giant nets and thrown away like garbage into a hostile desert, making it impossible to re-enter the country to fight again as it was barricaded by high steel gates and heavily armed soldiers.

"We survive by using our animal instinct," Arvid explained. "And we aren't the only ones. There are thousands of former Baraktenians like us living in the desert as we speak, roaming around mindlessly."

"As small brown hairy things with sharp teeth and very smelly farts," Rox added.

"The cruelty of it," Jet said.

"You got that right," Arvid agreed. "I'd dearly love to see her jailed and the key thrown away. Better still, she could be turned into a pig herself – see how she likes it."

"This food here's better than sex," Rox said, suddenly changing the subject. "I never fancied eating ants and spiders that much. Even as an animal."

"So the three of you have a disability of some kind?" Jet asked conversationally.

"Arvid's partially blind, Amus has a limp and I got an extra finger," Rox said, holding his hand up for Jet to see. "Apparently it makes me 'blemished' but I'm kind of fond of it, ya know?"

"How do you cope with now being half-animal?"

"There are pros and cons," Arvid replied. "We're able to survive by instinct and we can breathe underground, but the animal force can overtake us when we're really angry and when that happens, we remain in the animal state for hours at a time, whether we want to or not."

"But you can obviously turn human at will too," Jet said.

"Yes," Arvid agreed. "But most of the time we choose to remain in the animal state. It's not as aesthetically pleasing but it makes it a damned lot easier, as the animal inside us instinctively knows so much more about survival than the human does."

"I can't wait to take you to Sarakonia," Jet said. "You'll be able to put the past behind you, terrible as it was. Meet new people, settle down…"

He could see their faces light up as he spoke.

"I wanna hear more about this country," Rox said enthusiastically. "Tell me everything while you give me yer wine. Go on man – I can listen all night!"

"Gladly," he replied as he handed over the wineskin.

Two Hours Later

There was still no sign of Amus but the three men had forgotten all about him anyway, lost in hours of lively conversation and laughter. As the night wore on though, Rox eventually tired of conversation that didn't particularly interest him. He soon fell asleep listening to Jet and Arvid droning on about boring-as-bat-shit books and even worse, philosophy.

While his friend snored noisily on the ground nearby, Arvid spontaneously reached for Jet's strong brown hand and boldly squeezed it. "I just wanted to say thank you. I've been craving a conversation like this for a very long time."

"Yes," Jet agreed. "I felt that strongly in you."

"My companions aren't especially intelligent or well-read men."

"No, they're not. Although there's a bond there from shared misfortunes, you'll never fit in with them completely. I feel a deep loneliness in you, a frustration."

Arvid felt relieved to finally be understood. "I'm so glad I met you – that I convinced the boys not to eat you. The pig teeth we've been given are razor sharp – they could've torn you apart very easily, you know. For once, I managed to get them to listen to me. Usually they don't."

"But you wanted me alive. You wanted to spare me."

Arvid smiled. "You said you wanted to talk. I starve for words much more than I do food, my friend." He paused. "There was another reason…"

"What was that?"

The tone of the half-man, half-pig suddenly became much softer. "Come now," he teased. "You've shown yourself to be a psychic; don't you already know the answer to that question?"

There was an even longer pause; they stared at each other.

"One thing I do know: your loneliness is shortly coming to its end," Jet said meaningfully.

Barakten
Queen's Chamber
Yella Speaks

The officials paid me another visit that night and when they finally left, the gut-wrenching fear sank all the way to my bones.

I paced restlessly between Queen Elsbeth's enormous bed and her even more enormous windows.

We'll give you another chance, they said, and you must not fail this time as you will be executed. We'll meet with you tomorrow morning. Thirty soldiers have already been discharged to retrieve the Queen and they're travelling through the Baraktenian Desert as we speak...

So much for trance, I thought. *So much for helping people. How was I supposed to psychically tune in with repeated threats of hanging? With images of birds pecking at my dead eyeballs? I gave them everything I had; what the hell was I supposed to do? Wave a magic wand and suddenly make her appear, like I was a Goddam fairy or something? Was that what they expected?*

I flopped on the bed with my stomach firmly in knots, staring miserably at the ceiling.

Baraktenian Desert

Steele Silver laid under the glistening stars with half-closed eyes, a dreamy smile and a hardening cock. He was naked, lying blissfully on top of a blanket, with a fellow sorcerer named Lissette, who was also naked, lying blissfully on top of *him.*

She leisurely teased his nipples with her tongue for a while as her hands roamed freely, long, delicate fingers spreading and sliding along the landscape of his chest. Then she travelled further, gripping the sides of his head as she eagerly sought to explore him, firmly pushing a probing pink tongue in his mouth as she kissed. And kissed... And kissed... He groaned appreciatively as he slid his hands down her back and firmly grabbed her bottom, rubbing and kneading lustily as the desire in him climbed steadily upwards. She was so soft - so silky soft, and that mouth! That lovely, lovely, mouth…

Lissette had always been great with her mouth, and whatever body part it concentrated on immediately lit up and sprang and pulsed with life. A short time later, it concentrated on the most crucial body part of all: she clamped down firmly on his thickness as she rhythmically and methodically began to suck. Oh God. He closed his eyes in complete surrender as she took him deeply, riding on rising waves of lust, feeling wonderful sensations of heat and moisture and–

"Dear God!" Lissette said in disgust, pulling away from him. "I just felt a hairy hand on my bottom!"

"And it's not mine?" he asked, sitting up on his elbows.

"I refuse to stay here," she announced sourly. "Take me somewhere *else* next time."

Before he knew it, Lissette had disappeared and he was suddenly face to face with a sand monster, waist-deep in the earth and staring at him blankly. He quickly slapped it hard across the face, the force of which left it badly dazed, nearly unconscious. It slumped forward immediately. With the speed of a snake, he grabbed its wrist with both hands, twisting it cruelly, feeling the bone snap as it broke. The animal howled in agony as it quickly sank back into the ground, defeated.

"Goddammit!" Steele said angrily. "Ruining my sex life! I should have killed you, you miserable, pathetic, fang-faced, hairy-assed bastard!"

Sand monsters looked a bit like giant humans covered in brown fur. Apart from being exceedingly vicious, they were around seven feet tall and had pointy ears, pug noses and a very nasty set of claws and fangs. They were incredibly muscular and powerful, their fangs and claws easily slicing through human flesh. They and their snotty-nosed, smelly offspring swarmed in the Baraktenian Desert, living underground and eating anything they could lay their filthy, hairy hands on, an unfortunate fact of life in the place. He personally found them a huge pain in the ass.

"Try that again and I'll rip your miserable arm clear from its socket! Do we understand each other?" he yelled at the ground.

Unfortunately he failed to react to the sand monster in time when it responded to that statement. It shot out of the earth like a rocket, slapping him hard across the face with its remaining well-functioning hand before sinking down into the ground again.

"Ow!" Steele shouted. "Hairy bastard! You think you're so clever, don't you?"

A hand immediately shot up from the ground, and he swore it made a very rude gesture at him before sinking down again but it was hard to tell in the dark. If he hadn't been such a powerful sorcerer, the creature could have easily pulled him down into the sandy earth, dragged him to an underground cave and torn into his flesh, eating him alive. It probably would have engaged in pleasant feral chit-chat, a nice cup of tea and a good laugh while it was at it too. Maybe even shared him around with a few of its feral aunties and uncles, just to be nice. It happened to some other poor bastards out there.

But not him. He was special. He was a sorcerer. He could do magic. He was three-hundred-and-fifty-two-years-old and looked twenty-eight. He wore a beard and had thick, dark-brown wavy hair and bright yellow eyes.

The eyes were a distinguishing feature, but at the same time they were not at all unique. All sorcerers had them; it was an indelible mark of their kind. Besides the eyes, he was pleasant enough looking, but nothing to write home about. His usual garb (when not in Sarakonia) was a long black robe and sandals.

He had a triple life: one, as a sorcerer who liked to move between Sarakonia and the Baraktenian Desert a lot because he was hyperactive; two, as a professional stallholder in the Sarakonian markets who managed to hold down a regular job selling jewelry a few days a week; and three, as a big, ugly crow that resided chiefly in the Baraktenian Desert, doing birdy un-human things.

He also enjoyed managing a hospital in the Baraktenian Desert for lost and injured stragglers, but the need for that didn't arise very often.

His life as a bird was definitely a lot simpler and more peaceful than his human life, but it could also be a lot duller. He needed to experience both forms, so he shape-shifted often from bird to man and vice-versa.

His romantic life also varied. He had a long-term girlfriend named Three, whom he loved dearly and lived with in the Sarakonian mountains, but he often bedded other women, as his restless nature demanded it. He was not overly bright; in fact he had the attention span of an excitable gnat, but he was very powerful and that, to him, more than compensated for any short-comings.

He was a sorcerer after all. He could do magic, and that took him to the very top of the tree. No – far beyond; it took him to the furthest reaches of space, and as far as he was concerned the entire universe could kiss his lily-white ass. Including sand monsters.

Elsewhere in the Desert

After experiencing the most mind-blowing orgasm he'd ever had in his life, Arvid groaned, went cross-eyed, and fell backward and butt-naked onto the ground, quickly turning into a pig before he died.

Nearby his friend Rox shortly followed – his snoring stopped for the very last time before he too shape-shifted back into animal form and became one with eternity.

Jet, still kneeling on the ground, casually wiped traces of Arvid's sperm from his mouth as he observed the scene, hardly believing his luck. Magic worked in strange ways – even death couldn't cause a sorcerer's magic to break its powerful hold. It was great news for him, for not only would the poison he planted in their food be fully out of their bodies within a matter of minutes, he now had two fat, juicy pigs to keep him replenished – nicely flavored with a little wine.

He'd thoroughly enjoyed having poor little Arvid – he'd been a wild ride. The pig/man ex-librarian had been a noisy, passionate and responsive lover, writhing and bucking around like a lusty maggot at his touch, eager to feel, explore and please in any way he could – and go back for seconds too. Excitable and insatiable, it was like he'd go on screwing forever if death hadn't stopped him.

Obviously words weren't the only thing he'd been starved of.

But the pig men were still only novices in the ways of the Baraktenian Desert, whilst he'd been travelling and living in it for the last fifteen years. And if there was one simple rule of survival he'd learned more than anything else, it was this: kill or be killed.

He had no choice but to kill the pig men – they couldn't be trusted to keep to their promise of not killing him. It was a shame, as he'd really liked all of them (even the surly Amus), but that, unfortunately, was the way it was.

Since he was still hungry, he decided to cook and eat two pig legs that night, then conserve the rest of the meat for the following day. He spared a few seconds to gaze casually at the two very dead pigs in front of him before preparing their bodies.

"Never mess with strange men travelling alone in deserts my friends, for you are very tasty with sauce," he joked.

Chapter Two

Barakten
Queen's Chamber
Yella Speaks

I was still staring at the ceiling when I felt a strong presence sitting next to me and immediately became afraid. I turned my head to see who or what it was, and my eyes widened.

"Grandmother!" I sat up excitedly.

"This place reeks with the stench of death," she said, screwing up her nose in revulsion. "Get out of here. Don't wait for morning to come. They don't trust you. They plot against you even as we speak, and I'm afraid they'll…" She started to fade.

"Don't go," I protested.

"I have to go. And you have to act," she warned, coming into focus again.

"Stay with me a while."

"I was a frail old woman," she reminded me. "You knew you wouldn't have me on this earth forever."

"But I've really missed you. Can't you stay a while longer?"

"I've had my time. Don't waste yours fussing over dead women. And incidentally I love you too. Now if you don't wish to join me, I suggest you stop dilly-dallying and get on with it."

"But I'm in a palace surrounded by armed guards," I pointed out. "How am I supposed to escape?"

"Meditate," she said simply, then vanished.

When I woke from the dream, there was no doubt in my mind that my grandmother had visited me in spirit to warn me. And I knew how to meditate well, being a very experienced meditator – I did it every day without fail, sometimes for hours at a time. But it's hard to still the mind when the heart's beating so wildly, and the thoughts are racing through the head, demanding to be heard.

But I knew I had to try. I forced myself to start the process, asking my higher self to show me the way out of there. I relaxed my body as much as I could, starting from my head and working my way down. Then I started concentrating on my breath.

Breath rising.

Breath falling.

Rising.

Falling.

Rising.

Falling.

Rising.

Falling.

And on and on it went. When I finally got lost in the great rhythm of breath, it was as if time had ceased to exist and there I was, sucked into a vacuum of nothingness again; a wonderful vacuum of nothingness, where everything was so peaceful and so still, and before I knew it, I'd returned to the deep well: to trance.

Once my mind broke free of its shackles it started to wander, travelling outside the palace walls of Barakten, through the noise, lights and figures walking on the streets, past the great city gates and the armed guards, seeing nothing but darkness, moonlight and stars above and sand and grass below. I ventured further, moving fast, past more bushes, clumps of grass, spiders, snakes, ants, more grass, until…

Hello! Who have we here? a man asked telepathically.

Sweet Lord! I'm sorry! I was travelling. You were in the way, I telepathed back.

That I was, he answered. *I feel your presence strongly. Who are you?*

My name's Yella Fella.

In my mind's eye I saw a lone, dark-haired man sitting cross-legged inside a tent, bare-chested and eyes closed, illuminated by the firelight outside. He was a psychic, just like me, and he'd been meditating too.

Our telepathic connection was crystal clear and absolutely striking. The thoughts ran between us at blinding speed, even overlapping at times. The stranger's name was Jet Black and he was a spice merchant from Sarakonia, on his way to Barakten to trade. When I told him about the Queen being kidnapped, it blew him away.

Queen Elsbeth? Kidnapped? He paused. *You sure about this?*

I saw it. She just vanished, and no-one saw her go. But I did, in my mind's eye. I saw them take her–

Where?

To a jail in Sarakonia.

I'll be damned!

I told the court officials. They've sent thirty armed soldiers to go to Sarakonia to get her back, and they're crossing the desert as we speak. They want more information from me about her, but it won't come. I've tried everything. I didn't please them before and they threatened to kill me.

Get out of there. I've a strong feeling they'll kill you if you stay. There are too many who don't trust you; powerful people. Get out of there, he repeated, sounding very firm.

But I can't leave, I protested. *There's no way. I'm under armed guard.*

There's always a way, my friend. It's only waiting to be found.

What are you talking about?

Ten Minutes Later

I came back to full consciousness with a shocking jolt as large chunks of glass and concrete crashed to the ground and skidded across the floor. Then I saw the same leathery, four-legged creature I'd seen earlier in my vision: a studdgarta. It'd smashed its way through the locked bedroom window with blinding speed and was now sitting at the foot of the Queen's bed, looking at me expectantly with its green, slitted eyes.

Not exactly subtle, but very efficient.

Then I heard sounds of heavy footsteps running along the corridor and there was no time left to think. I quickly jumped onto its back as it lurched, then leaped out the window. I pressed myself hard against its back and held tightly onto its neck, praying the gunshots I heard behind me would miss. The creature was smart – it was travelling at top speed, artfully dodging the hail of bullets by flying in zigzags. I looked down and saw the city lights shining like pin pricks below me and gritted my teeth as I held on, heart thumping fast.

Another Ten Minutes Later
Baraktenian Desert

I feel you. You're close. Very close, Jet telepathed.

Sweet Lord I hope so! I answered, clinging like hell to the studdgarta's neck as we tore through the skies.

His voice came into my head amongst the black sky and freezing winds – I had no clue how high up I was. All I knew was that I was crapping my pants and wanted my feet back on the ground more than anything. I ached from holding onto the studdgarta so hard, I was frozen to the core of my bones and I was terrified, praying to make it to the desert ground alive and in one piece.

Looking down, I saw a tiny bright dot shining in the darkness and guessed it was Jet's campfire. Sure enough, the studdgarta tore down towards it while I hung onto its neck for dear life. It landed so roughly I fell off it, and sand flew everywhere as I landed straight on my face.

"Greetings, Yella," Jet said cheerfully. "Did you enjoy your flight?"

I lifted my head up to look at him, spat the sand out of my mouth, and groaned in misery. It seemed every part of my body was throbbing and pulsing.

He laughed. He was sitting close to the campfire, looking calm and relaxed as he chewed heartily on a meat bone. "Survival often gets in the way of comfort, doesn't it?" He stood up and threw the remains of his bone to the studdgarta. "Good boy," he told it as it caught the bone in its mouth and flew off into the night sky.

I rolled onto my back and he walked towards me till he stood over me like a tower.

"In case you're wondering, I communicated with the studdgarta telepathically to get you," he said as I slowly sat up from the ground. "I already know who you are. In fact, I've been hearing about you for years. Apparently you're a great psychic talent? Well they could be right about that," he shrugged. "But talent, like everything else, has its limits."

He took a handgun out from his back pocket and to my absolute horror, pointed it straight at me. "Feelings have a nasty habit of blocking the psychic sense; of getting in its way," he said. "You know that, don't you? If you weren't so scared, you would've known to stay away from me. You would've picked up on the thoughts I hid from you."

I stared at him in disbelief. "I trusted you."

"Trust is a dirty word," he scoffed. "It's for idiots with short lives. Trust no-one. Especially strange men travelling alone in deserts like me."

"Why?"

"I don't like your Queen very much. She's wasted thousands of lives with her stupid banishment policy. Can you picture that? Thousands of lives. It's a lot of waste, isn't it?" His gun clicked menacingly as he pointed it at me. "I don't like waste."

"Please," I begged.

"How do you think I feel about the scum that support her, eh? And not only support her, but rally thirty fucking soldiers to get her back?"

"I had no choice," I stammered. "If I didn't help them, they would've killed me."

"Don't give me your bullshit," he sneered. "There's always a choice. And you'll die for making this one."

❧

Sarakonia
The Mountains

The sorcerer and psychic Crimson Velvet suddenly sat bolt upright and naked in bed, her large yellow eyes nearly popping out of their sockets. "Oh, my stars!"

She was a one-hundred-and-three-year-old woman who looked around twenty, with a pretty face, pale skin, slim build, and shoulder-length, curly blonde hair. She quickly woke her husband lying beside her – Cory, a stocky, bearded hunter and ordinary mortal man, with no powers at all and no interest in attaining any either.

"What's wrong, dear?" he asked, groggily sitting up.

"I saw them in my dream as clear as day. They're coming for her."

"Eh?" he asked, still half asleep. "Who's coming for who?"

"The soldiers for Rebel Red," she explained. "The damned gossips – they've leaked her whereabouts. Oh, my stars. They come for her as we speak. She needs our help."

"Big surprise," Cory said, sounding bored. "What sort of fool escapes the Queen's army and thinks they can get away with it?"

"I'm not powerful enough to save her. I need Steele and Three to help me."

He rolled onto his side disinterestedly, used to his wife's peculiarities. "Have a good time, dear."

She curled her lip in irritation. How *supportive*. She then instantly shape-shifted into a hawk and once out the window, travelled fast, flying straight through the bedroom window of her fellow sorcerers and good friends, Three and her rather arrogant boyfriend, Steele Silver. It was a short trip, as they weren't that far; they just lived in another part of the Sarakonian mountains.

"Three! Steele! Wake up, I beg you!" she shouted, perching herself on top of a bed sheet between the two sorcerers. Her best friend, an attractive woman with generous breasts and long waves of thick, auburn hair, woke with a jolt, along with her partner Steele. She was one-hundred-and-eighty-six-years-old and looked around twenty-five. They both sat up, naked and dazed.

Steele in particular was unimpressed. "Crimson," he muttered irritably. "What the hell do you think you're doing?"

She spoke very fast, looking from one sorcerer to the other. "Rebel Red is in trouble. The Baraktenian soldiers have discovered her whereabouts. The run-down excuse for a house she lives in – they've been told where it is. They're coming for her this very evening; they may even be there already. I have seen it in my dream, and I also feel it in the core of my bones. We *must* help her."

"Crimson Crimson Crimson," Steele scolded, half-asleep and running his fingers through his hair in exasperation. "This is totally inappropriate. One, she was an idiot to escape from the Baraktenian army in the first place; two, it is none of our business; and three, you know full well it is against our Code of Conduct to interfere in the lives of mortals."

"She is a very good friend of ours and her life happens to be in mortal danger as we speak," Crimson argued. "I beg you to bend the rules and use your powers, just this once, to help."

He rolled his eyes. "Correction: she's friends with yourself and Three, not I. I've never even met the woman. This is pathetic, Crimson. Pathetic. You girls should be more careful of the filthy riff-raff you are so fond of picking up on the streets. Will that be all?"

Crimson stared at him, fighting off a sudden, powerful urge to slap his arrogant face as hard as she could. She first met the twenty-eight-year-old Baraktenian ex-soldier in a tavern while she was on an army training expedition in Sarakonia. Rebel was not riff-raff, but she could certainly look intimidating: a profusion of tattoos and silver jewelry adorned her toned and super-fit body, and her black soldier's uniform was a mish mash of buckles, leather, cloth and boots. Her shoulder-length, dark-brown hair was shaved at the sides and artfully tamed into a tight, orderly braid that fell slightly past her shoulders.

Yes, she thought, *Rebel definitely looks, shall we say, 'different', but she is no troublemaker.* On the contrary, she found her to be a very sweet and loyal friend; a friend she did not want to lose, Code of Conduct or no Code of Conduct.

"I have not come to discuss the subject of riff-raff. I have come to help Rebel," Crimson said evenly. "And time is running short," she added, impatiently stamping her bird leg on the bed. "Please help, I beg you. We will be saving a life that's important to me, and you are both fully aware that I'm unable to do this on my own."

The magical pecking order was clear in their friendship. Steele was exceedingly powerful, Three less so but still impressive, and she – well, she had a lot to learn, and though she attempted to improve on her abilities, she was still a complete and utter magical weakling in comparison. The only thing she seemed to possess that they did not was psychic talent, but that ability could be a double-edged sword. Sometimes it could be a curse to know the future, but in this case she hoped it would be a blessing. She hoped it would save a dear friend's life.

"I happen to be very fond of *sleeping*, my dear. Especially when I'm tired. Count me out," Steele replied sourly, lying back in bed and rolling onto his side.

Crimson wasn't stupid enough to argue with Steele in a bad mood. "Three?" she turned to her best friend pleadingly.

Three stared at her with her bright yellow eyes for what seemed like an eternity, before finally rolling them and appearing to give up. "She owes me a drink for this," she sighed in resignation, roughly pushing her bed sheet away.

"Goddammit," was the last word out of Steele's mouth before he finally fell into a deep sleep, snoring without a care in the world.

~~~

Barakten
A Run-Down House in a Poor Street

"Holy fuck!" were the first words out of Rebel's mouth when she woke up in the middle of the night to find two powerful sorcerers in nighties shaking the shit out of her.

"Good evening Rebel. It's lovely to see you," Crimson said cheerfully. Both women had put on long, white nightgowns for modesty, though they needn't have bothered, as their gowns were flimsy and their nakedness underneath obvious.

"Whassup? Whassup?" Rebel kept on repeating, rolling her head from side to side, half-dazed from sleep. Anybody else would've gotten a steady mouthful of obscenities for the audacity of waking her up in the middle of the night, maybe even a well-aimed punch in the face, but these women were her friends and even more important, very powerful sorcerers; she was smart enough to watch her mouth around them.

"We've come to save your life," Crimson announced.

"The soldiers are coming to get you," Three added casually, as if Rebel and the Baraktenian army had a pleasant date for afternoon tea. "They will be here very soon, so I suggest you get dressed and prepare to escape. Hurry now."

This got an immediate reaction from Rebel, who forgot she was tired and sleepy and sprang out of bed like she'd just been poked with a hot iron rod. "Where're my clothes?"

Crimson turned to her best friend while the ex-soldier scrounged around the floor in a panic, trying to find scattered clothes and shoes in the dark. "We've frightened her," she observed. "We probably should have been more organized about this and checked the skies *before* waking her up, to see exactly how far away the soldiers are."

Three shrugged. "I'll check now."

Despite her fear, Rebel froze in awe as Three shape-shifted to a great eagle, repeatedly flapped her gigantic wings on the spot, forced the bedroom window open by magic, and flew with amazing speed into the steamy night air.

Sure enough, after doing a rough circle of the skies at fifty feet for about five minutes, she spotted exactly what she had been expecting to see – the unmistakable glare of motorbike headlights travelling towards Rebel's house.

Just minutes later there was a firm knock on the front door, sending Rebel's heart pounding and her blood turn cold. Forcing herself to stay calm, she motioned to Crimson to be silent by bringing a finger to her lips as she tiptoed out of her bedroom and crept along the corridor, slowly pulling a gun out of her hip holster as she did so. Crimson nervously followed, praying that if it were soldiers, there would only be a few of them. She could handle a few soldiers with her powers, but any more than that, well...

In a flash Rebel opened the door, slammed a woman with long blonde hair against the wall and held a gun to her head. "Who the fuck are you?" she demanded, brown eyes flashing dangerously.

The blonde woman, in total fear and shock, was pulling all sorts of weird faces and was struggling to speak. "I...I want to go to Sarakonia and I need a guide," she stammered when she finally managed to find her voice.

"Is anyone with you?"

"No."

"Then how'd you know I was here?"

"*Everybody* knows you're here."

"Dammit!" Rebel stated in disgust. "Can no-one in this God-forsaken street keep their fucking mouth shut?"

"I...I need a guide," the blonde woman repeated, terrified but stubborn. "I heard you have experience and—"

"A guide? You should take her up on that," Crimson suggested, standing behind her in the corridor. "I believe Sarakonia is the only logical place for you to go right now."

"I wanna stay where I belong, and that's not in Sarakonia," Rebel said. More relaxed in the blonde woman's presence now but still cautious, she released her and put her gun back in her hip holster.

"You must be more realistic, my dear," Crimson argued. "You'll never be safe in this country again – not after what you've done. Besides, I believe you already know how to get to Sarakonia from Barakten – from all the training expeditions you've been on?"

"I'm an ex-soldier – I've been around."

"You know I'm right, don't you? I see it in your eyes. Deep down in your heart, you know I'm right."

"Yeah you're right," Rebel admitted, feeling defeated. "You're always right."

"Then it would be better to travel with company, would it not? She looks like a perfectly nice girl to me."

"She looks like she drinks fine tea and eats puff cakes," Rebel muttered irritably. "She'd only slow me down."

"I'll pay money," the blonde woman squeaked.

Rebel raised her eyebrows. "Then where is it?"

The blonde woman shakily reached inside her robe, pulled out a thick wad of notes from her trouser pocket, and waved it around triumphantly in front of Rebel's face. "As you can see, I'm not bluffing. Do you mind if I use your toilet now, please?"

Five Minutes Later

When Three flew through the kitchen window and shape-shifted back to human form, she saw Crimson sitting at a table with a woman she'd never seen before. The woman, a pretty blonde, was softly illuminated by oil lamps strategically placed around the room and was clutching a knapsack to her chest like her life depended on it. She promptly let out a very unpleasant, ear-shattering scream when she saw her shape-shift, so she was obviously human.

"I've been gone less than ten minutes and you start making new friends. My dear Crimson, it seems as if you're trying to replace me," she joked as she walked purposefully down the corridor towards Rebel's bedroom.

"She was at the door so we–" Crimson began, hurrying to the window to close and lock it.

"No time for idle chit-chat I'm afraid," Three said over her shoulder. "Rebel," she said, opening the door to the soldier's bedroom. "Come over here at once. I need to speak with you."

The ex-soldier, who'd been frantically dressing and packing supplies, practically sprinted towards her as Three motioned her to the corridor.

"They will be here any minute, according to my calculations," Three said calmly.

Rebel momentarily froze on the spot, staring at her in complete horror. "Then I gotta get outta here."

She abruptly turned to go, but Three firmly gripped her arm and stopped her. "No," she insisted, a fierce look of reproach blazing in her eyes. "You must wait until I do magic on you first."

"Are you crazy?" Rebel protested, gesturing wildly with her hands. "There's no time!"

Three held Rebel's chin firmly in her fingers and looked her straight in the eyes. "Calm yourself, dear one. Their guns cannot hurt me," she murmured.

"But they can me."

"I will protect you," she said. "I have personally faced much larger enemies…will you not trust me?"

"Alright Three," Rebel said tersely, hoping to hurry her along, "I trust you."

Rebel had many virtues, but patience wasn't one of them. She longed to take ahold of Three's shoulders and shake her till her muscles ached, scream till she was hoarse that her life was in danger and to release her, but her gut instincts were telling her to be still, to shut up and do what she was told, that Three knew what she was doing despite there being no immediate proof of it. She could ignore anything and everything but never gut instincts; they were a soldier's artillery.

Three gazed at her steadily with her freakish yellow eyes. "Such an innocent to sorcery," she murmured. "You know only of guns, and what you can see and touch, and the way of men, but not the way of magic. Magic is another world altogether…let me show you. Don't. Move," she warned, still keeping her gaze firmly fixed on the soldier.

She took a single step back and held her arms out, palms pointing towards Rebel's body, and the powerful but invisible magic flowed in and around her as it quickly took hold. Rebel didn't feel a thing, much less any magical force, but submitted obediently to her friend, even though her heart hammered in her chest and her legs felt so weak they barely managed to support her. She closed her eyes and bravely waited for Three to give her more instructions, despite feeling ugly waves of terror and nausea wash over her.

After about a minute, Three dropped her arms. "You will not be seen or heard for twenty-four hours. That goes for your supplies, your friend and anything else around you. That should do it," she said, looking very satisfied with herself. "That should save you. And incidentally it's a little dark in here, don't you think?" she added, slicing a hand in the air. Torchlights instantly lit up the walls, uncomfortably heating the house at the same time.

"Can't you just, you know, kill them all to get them off my back?" Rebel asked.

"Not directly," Three said, shaking her head. "Intentional killing drains the magical energy too much. I usually slam people against things with my force, and that often ends up killing them anyway."

The ex-soldier's eyes widened. "How–"

She never got to finish that sentence as the front door was forcibly kicked open and a male voice shouted, "Put your hands up!"

Three instinctively picked Rebel up by the collar, quickly throwing her to the ground to protect her, and as Rebel rolled out of harm's way, Three felt a spray of bullets that didn't even cause her to flinch – the metal just bounced continuously off her body as if they were little fleas.

As Rebel desperately tried to crawl her way to safety, Three went to work, and the incredible energetic force streaming from her opened palm hit eight burly men, sending them hurtling backwards through the air like fragile little dolls. She then sprinted to the kitchen, where she found the blonde woman and Crimson screaming and huddling together under a table.

"Crimson!" she shouted. "What the hell are you doing? You're supposed to be helping me!"

"I cannot hold them, Three! I cannot hold them!" she screamed. Her face was bright red, she was shaking and tears were streaming down her cheeks. "I'm not strong enough!"

There was a mighty racket as the kitchen window above them shattered under the weight of gunfire. Two more armed soldiers were attempting to get into the house.

"Out!" Three barked, pointing an opened palm at them as they screamed and flew back from her force. With no time left for the luxury of thinking, Three spun around in a circle so fast she was nothing but a blur of movement, a swirling mass that soon split into three people running in different directions: one to the bedroom, one to the corridor, and one closer to the kitchen window.

The next five minutes were messy and ear-splittingly loud as Three and her two clones turned into lethal savages, thirsty for action and blood. They weren't disappointed in that department, as more and more armed soldiers poured their way through the house's orifices, charging at the inhabitants like a gang of mad sewer rats. Torchlights came off their hinges and fell to the ground as bodies flew and crashed through walls, going dead before they dropped. The building started to burn. There were more gunshots. More screams and cries. More bodies slammed through walls, flying through windows or running out with clothes and hair set ablaze.

Meanwhile Rebel made good use of both her time and her invisibility, skillfully dodging the flying bodies and bullets as she finished the last of her packing, stole a bike from a soldier, and collected a rich blonde passenger before finally driving off. And all while keeping her heart rate steady and her body in one piece!

It was the most magnificent, athletic display of efficiency ever, even if she did say so herself, and it was almost a crime that her former squadron leader wasn't there to witness it. He would've given her top marks, maybe even a medal; and then she would've shot his ass (because he was a prick).

Little did she know that Three had managed to kill all of the soldiers – every single one, without so much as a scratch – and with no help whatsoever from her friend Crimson Velvet.

Even though Rebel rode through the cobbled streets at top speed, it still took a decent ten minutes to reach the great gates that bordered their country, flanked by two armed guards that only ever opened the gates for travelling merchants. She reached them just as they were about to close, expertly dodging a merchant in front of her on the way.

"Stop!" the blonde woman shouted, looking at the closing gates in alarm. "Are you mad? We won't make it! We'll crash!"

Rebel ignored her and went for it, just making it through with only inches to spare. And then the great gates closed with finality as the two women left their lives in their homeland behind forever – one laughing and whooping like an insane lunatic in victory, the other one screaming at the top of her lungs.

***

Baraktenian Desert
Yella Speaks

You're dead!

As soon as Jet uttered those telepathic words to me, a man shot up from the ground behind him. He was carrying a large rock in his hands and brought it down hard against the back of his head, knocking him out cold.

"I *knew* he didn't smell right," he said as Jet dropped at his feet.

"Who are you?" I demanded, quickly taking in his physicality: a young man, long hair, brown eyes, stocky build.

He ignored me and picked up the gun lying on the sandy ground.

"No! Don't kill him!" I yelled, quickly getting up.

We struggled with the gun as we argued.

"Why not, you dumb bastard?" he spat breathlessly. "He just tried to kill you, didn't he? He just killed two of the only fucking friends I had left in the world and now I'm alone!"

"What happened?"

We momentarily stopped struggling as we looked at each other, still keeping a firm grip on the gun.

"He ate them!" he replied, wild-eyed and hysterical. "You saw it with your own fucking eyes! You saw him eating the meat!"

"He only ate wild pig," I gasped.

"They were my *friends*, you fuckwit!"

We continued struggling.

"Don't kill him! You'll pay the wages for it in this life or the next!" I said, trying to talk some sense into him. "It's...bad karma!"

He spat in my face, then viciously head-butted me on the nose. "That's what I think of you and your fucking karma! We're all doomed anyway!"

I reeled back from the blow, immediately feeling sharp pain and warm blood gush from my nostrils. Out of the corner of my eye I saw him dive into the ground, vanishing quickly into the desert earth, and then I was left with nothing but an eerie silence.

Dizzy, gasping, and with a bloody nose, I spun around defensively, as if something or someone was going to shoot up out of the ground at any second and get me. Even the silence seemed evil and threatening somehow, like it was containing something that was about to explode. I fought off a powerful urge to grab the bike sitting nearby and just get out of there. Tear off fast. But the next day, and the pressing issue of food and water loomed.

I had to survive.

I had to use my brains.

I had to pack.

Sweet Lord, I had to pack!

Wiping my bloody nose with my sleeve, I shook my head back to reality, deciding to tie up the spice merchant first in case he came to and tried to attack me again. I moved as fast as I could, but it still took at least fifteen minutes to tie him up, gather and load his supplies, and turn the bike on.

I'd ridden a bike before, but I still fiddled with the gears and controls with trembling hands and breathed a big sigh of relief when the engine suddenly roared to life.

And I rode, with the noisy engine cutting through the desert silence like a knife and the bright lights strongly illuminating the ground beneath and around me. I prayed to God I was going in the right direction; anywhere but Barakten sounded good. How long would I survive out here, I wondered, with only a few rations? Before I could find someone to help me? And what if I found no one?

I thought of Jet lying unconscious on the ground, waking up to what was surely going to be a slow and cruel death, and tried to shut out the guilt that was beginning to crawl its way through me. Sweet Lord, I just condemned a man to eternity! Me, the peaceful psychic, me, whose only ambition in life had been to help people, had just turned into me, the cold-blooded murderer.

And that wasn't the only insanity; the spice merchant was tied up, unconscious and as helpless as a baby with no food, water or transport to keep him alive, but I was still afraid he'd somehow find a way to get to me.

I argued with myself over his predicament. I kept telling myself to stay positive; that there was still a reasonable chance that he wouldn't die. Soldiers and merchants go through this desert all the time, I told myself; gangs as well. Maybe one of them would find him and take pity on him?

I forced myself to think of something else, so I indulgently thought of the Queen. If by some miracle I managed to get to Sarakonia, I'd be looking forward to completing the assignment I was given to find her. But this time it'd be different, I told myself. It'd be on my own terms, not anyone else's.

I lost myself in more thoughts of the Queen, and another hour sailed by.

I decided that sleep would be a sensible idea, so I stopped and made camp. Initially sleep was impossible as adrenaline pumped through me, but it did come eventually and when it did, the dream I had started off nicely. I was no longer in a harsh desert – I was somewhere else, a wonderful place, a place of tall, leafy trees and lush green grass. The day was sunny and warm and the water inviting.

In a good mood, I stripped off all my clothes, ran towards the water and dived in, enjoying the feel of the water on me as I swam. As I treaded water about fifty meters away from the riverbank, I saw a man in the distance watching me, sitting on the grass. I knew instantly who it was, and the fear struck like a bolt of lightning as our conversation began.

"Did you miss me?"

He got up and started walking towards me and when he reached the water's edge, he didn't stop; he kept right on walking. The water was holding him as if it were earth beneath his feet.

"You look familiar somehow. We've shared lifetimes, I can feel it," I said.

"So do I, but who gives a shit? I'm getting you good before you wake up."

"I'm dreaming?"

"Unless I've miraculously turned into a sorcerer who can walk on water, yes you are."

"Whaddaya think you're doing?" I shouted, punching at the water angrily. "Can't you leave things as they are without going into such a damned sulk about it? I had to do what I could to survive and if you were me, you would've done the same, don't deny it!"

Jet suddenly stopped walking and pointed at me menacingly. "Get fucked! You left me to rot and die in the stinking desert and thought you could get away with it!"

"Your death isn't guaranteed. Soldiers, merchants and gangs go through this desert all–"

"I'm tied up with inch thick ropes, you dick! I can't fucking move and I've got no food, no water, no transport and a splitting headache!"

"Well who knows what tomorrow will–"

"Shuttup! We both know I've had it! And mark my words, you'll pay the wages!"

"All I wanted was your help and you tried to–"

"Wait a minute..." He suddenly stopped walking and seemed thoughtful.

"What?"

"We fight like an old married couple. Did we fornicate in a previous life?"

The thought of doing *that* with *him* filled me with horror and my face twisted.

He shrugged. "Well never say never, but let's not speculate too much. Let's get to the point of my visit. I've bought a present for you," he said in an evil sing-song voice.

I watched in horror as he shape-shifted into a gigantic, long-legged, hairy black spider – the size of a house – before my very eyes. At this point I was trying like hell to wake my conscious mind up so the dream wouldn't go on and the prick wouldn't get what he wanted.

"Wake up! Wake up! Wake up!" I screamed to my conscious self in panic. "Sweet Lord! Wake up!"

"Not before I've had my fun, you won't." His eyes lit up with an evil glee. "Come to mama sweetheart, I'm feeling peckish."

I watched the hideous thing run towards me for about half a second before swimming like hell towards the other side of the river – big surprise, I didn't make it. It picked me up easily and turned me on my side and I felt giant fangs puncture into me, sinking deep, filling me with venom. Then I was paralyzed as my insides were being quickly sucked out – they were flowing away from me like a current, till nothing of me was left but a thin blanket of hanging skin.

Oh God!

I woke up trembling, still strongly feeling the sensation of my insides being sucked out and trying to hold them all together. For a few seconds of waking consciousness, it felt like they were going to spill over onto the ground at any second, but they didn't. They stayed exactly where they were, and I groaned and threw up instead.

Elsewhere in the Desert
The Following Day

Jet was too weak to telepathically summon any studdgarta to save him, so he had no choice but to accept his fate. After a long and deep meditation session he'd finally managed to let go, to face the prospect of his own death with complete and utter acceptance – a strange yet peaceful feeling. When he felt ready, he asked his higher self if it was his time and was surprised at the answer he got: *no, not yet.*

He felt the soldiers' presence around him long before they came to him in physical form. In a brief flicker of doubt, he wondered if the answer he received was just the voice of his wishful imagination. Then he heard the faint sound of motorbike engines in the distance and knew.

He remembered a strong male voice shouting, "Get him water! Now!"

It took days for him to fully recover, plenty of time for him to collect his thoughts and weave his tale to them, which went like this: he met Yella by chance in the desert as he was making his way to Barakten to trade, and generously shared his food and water supplies with him. Yella had escaped from the Queen's palace to avoid getting executed and had telepathically summoned a studdgarta to retrieve him and fly him to the desert.

He'd tried hard to convince Yella to return as a good citizen should, but he stubbornly refused to listen to reason. Later that night, Yella had repaid his kindness by knocking him unconscious, tying him up, stealing his transport and supplies, and ruthlessly leaving him to die a slow and painful death in the desert.

They not only believed him, they assured him they'd lead him back to his homeland of Sarakonia safely, as that was where they were going too. After a time, he adapted to their ways of living and they adapted to his. They insisted he help with practical matters every day, like setting up tents and preparing dinner; he insisted on time alone to meditate. Both parties were happy to oblige each other and the days passed without incident.

Till one evening after he meditated for three hours straight, and made some very interesting psychic discoveries.

⌒〜⌒

Elsewhere in the Desert
Yella Speaks

We always attract what we fear the most.

That's always been my theory anyway, and that theory came true when after days of travelling without any problems, my bike suddenly spluttered, hissed, whirred, vibrated, weakened and finally stopped and died.

Dammit!

I tried everything I could think of to get it going again – I poked and prodded every knob and button on the thing I could see, but nothing worked. I went through the supplies thoroughly, hoping to find some sort of tool that might help me, but found nothing. The bike really was dead, and there wasn't a thing I could do about it; it was like it'd just signed my death warrant with its leaking oil.

Out of sheer frustration, I kicked it hard and hurt my foot in the process. When I finally stopped swearing and hopping on one foot in agony, I sat down and stared at it as it lay forlornly on the ground, like the useless piece of metal crap that it was.

Sighing, I got down to business and carefully went through the supplies again, sorting out what I needed and what I didn't. I nearly cried when I discovered large amounts of crucial food supplies were missing – a bag must've come loose and fallen off the bike! I rummaged through what was left of the supplies and slung as much as I could in a single bag over my shoulder. It was heavy enough, but even so, it wouldn't last long. I surveyed the God-forsaken wasteland that lay before my eyes. Maybe I could travel by remote view that evening, to see what else was out there? It was worth a try. Anything was worth a try.

I forced myself to walk and despite eating small amounts of food, drinking water and resting when I felt tired, I felt my body steadily weakening. I went to bed exhausted that night and woke up the next day the same way.

Elsewhere in the Desert
Rebel Speaks

The blonde chick's name, I found out, was Petelia Rose – real pretty, with big blue eyes, a cute nose, and gorgeous long blonde hair. Twenty-one-years-old and a woman with many talents: she could sew, embroider, knit, recite poetry, sing, and play nice tunes on a piano. Apparently she was well-educated and rich too.

But her biggest talent by far was her God-given, natural ability to piss me off.

Apparently, she'd been in an unhappy marriage with some rich guy who used to beat her up and screw around on her. Whenever she'd try to leave him, he'd find her through contacts, then beat her up even more before dragging her ass back again. Is this poor taste in men, or what? I'd just shoot the fucker.

Alright, maybe that's a bit mean. Barakten's a pretty small country where everyone knows everyone – it's only got a population of around thirty thousand, and it's not like you can get out of it easily with tough-guy soldiers and a giant gate guarding its barriers, so I guess she didn't have that many options. If she wanted to stay alive, she had to get out of there.

But she sure likes to complain a lot, and I soon found out about *that* hobby – starting with our daily diet of desert root vegetables, which she absolutely hates. I show her how to collect root vegetables and which plants they come from; she complains she's tired and her back's hurting her. I show her which plant to draw water from; she complains the prickles on it are hurting her precious fingers. I try to teach her how to set up a tent and start a fire and she's completely useless at everything, so I give up and do it all myself while she sits on her butt and watches me with a bored look on her face.

I catch and kill a wild pig for dinner; she refuses to help me prepare it, saying she feels faint at the sight of blood, but she's more than happy to eat it after I've done all the work. Then at night while I'm finally trying to get some well-earned sleep, she snores. Really, really loudly.

I was starting to think, *what did I do to deserve this chick?* I knew I deserted an army and stole a man's bike and supplies, but was I really *that* much of an asshole?

I soon found out she wasn't much of a morning person either. I'd been trained for as long as I can remember to get up at the crack of dawn and that habit's been ingrained into me, so I got zero tolerance for those with no discipline.

On our second morning together she was still asleep, so I tried to wake her up by shaking her a little. There was no response.

After three more civilized attempts from me at waking her up and three more successful attempts from her at ignoring me, I was no longer in the mood for her crap. I shook her real rough and yelled at the top of my lungs, "Wake up!"

She sat up so fast, she nearly jumped out of her skin! If I wasn't so pissed off, I would've laughed.

"How dare you! How completely rude," she said indignantly, smoothing her messed up hair in place with her fingers.

"Get up! Not that hard to do!"

"Do you have to yell at me like that?"

"Yes I do, princess. You gotta get up when I tell you to."

"You've probably just damaged my ear drums for life," she bitched, cupping her palms against her ears.

"I won't tolerate slowness," I said sternly. "This is a dangerous desert we're travelling through and the quicker we get out of it, the better chance we have of survival. You got that?"

"You don't know what you're talking about," she said irritably. "There's nothing out here but sand and clumps of grass and… and…lousy root vegetables that taste like vile rat droppings." She screwed up her nose distastefully.

"I do know what I'm talking about, alright? I've been going on training expeditions through this desert since I was thirteen. There are animals that live under this ground, you know. And they're—"

"I'm not an idiot," she interrupted. "I know there are animals that live underground."

"These aren't the animals you know about. These are sand monsters. A lot of 'em are over seven feet tall. They usually rip you apart before eating you alive." I paused. "Sorry, that's not technically correct. They *gang-rape* you before ripping you apart, then eating you alive. They like to have a bit of fun first."

This would make any normal chick immediately throw up and wet her panties. She hardly reacted at all.

"Well goodness me, I haven't seen any so far," she said sarcastically.

"There's still time sweetheart, trust me. And not to mention the deadly spiders and snakes–"

"Do you have a first aid kit?" she said, suddenly looking alarmed.

"Do I have a vagina? Of course I have a first aid kit."

"Well, won't that fix it?"

"Some bites, yeah," I admitted. "But there's no antidote yet for the venom of certain species here, so we still need to be careful. Translate that as, 'get the fuck out of here fast'. Do you understand?" I gritted my teeth and glared at her.

She sighed, rolled her eyes, and appeared to back down. "Alright. I apologize, but I'm not exactly what you would call a morning person, and I'm not used to travelling either, like you obviously are. Can you make me a cup of tea please?"

I raised my eyebrows. "Who do you think I am? Your Goddam maid?"

"I used to have several maids."

"I don't see any maids around here. Do you?"

"I hate this God-forsaken, dirty place," she suddenly whined. "No-one should live like this. I'm as filthy as a rat."

"Yeah, sand gets stuck in the most unusual of places, doesn't it?"

"How about I pay you more money?" she offered, looking at me hopefully. "Then would you make me a cup of tea?"

"You can't afford me. Now you know where the supply bag is," I said, impatiently pointing outside the tent. "Make your own cup of tea and hurry up about it. I'm tired of waiting for you."

I walk off to start loading the bike, and she finally ventures outside for breakfast and morning tea. I left a small fire and boiling pot for her to make her breakfast with, and then as if she hadn't pissed me off enough, she took another shot.

"There's no need to be so snappy."

It was then I lost it. This woman was a complete asshole.

"You are so right!" I shouted. "Why waste my precious oxygen with words? Next time I won't bother with the lecture! I'll just pack up and leave without you! How would you like *that* for breakfast?"

One Hour Later

I spotted a lone figure walking in the far distance to our left as we were travelling on the bike and I made a point of checking him out. I'm glad I did; he looked exhausted and greatly relieved to see us.

"What the hell do you think you're doing out here by yourself with no bike?" were the first words that came out of my mouth once we'd come to a stop alongside him.

"I'm a spice merchant," he said, hair sticking out everywhere and looking like shit. "My bike died…I've got little food left, and almost no water. Please…can you help me?"

He looked young, in his early twenties. He was tall, with short, straight brown hair and a nice enough face, and I really liked his eyes. They were unusual: big, pale-blue, and full of expression.

"We most certainly will not," Petelia said flatly, electing to speak on my behalf.

"What are you talking about?" I asked, surprised that she'd suggest such a thing. "He'll *die* without our help."

"We can't afford to share our food and water around," she protested.

"Sweetheart, I've been on training expeditions in this desert with up to forty people and we've all managed perfectly well living off the land together," I countered.

"There's no room on the bike."

"He's no fatso. We'll manage."

"But he's a spice merchant," she argued. "Aren't they supposed to be experienced and clever? Adept in the ways of desert survival?"

The man, already exhausted and unsteady on his feet, collapsed and fainted in front of us.

"Apparently not," I replied.

Chapter Three

Three Days Later
Evening
Yella Speaks

I'll be forever grateful to the ex-soldier named Rebel Red for saving my life. She set up a tent and sheltered, fed and watered me, making sure I was strong enough to travel again. She said she wasn't on a tight schedule so a delay wouldn't matter. Just as well, as it took two full days to get back to normal again.

We were a dirty group – we stank like pigs and our bodies ached from lying on the hard desert ground at night. We squeezed in together, sharing a tent at night and a motorbike during the day. It wasn't exactly comfortable, but at least we were still alive, and that was all that mattered.

When the girls told me their names and backgrounds, I came clean about mine. They were as criminal as I was – two women illegally escaping their country, which we all knew was a crime punishable by death. One escaping a brutal army, the other escaping a brutal husband.

It was a nice change to be around people who didn't want to kill me and like me, had the goal of reaching Sarakonia and starting their life over. The extreme environment and circumstances we shared seemed to draw us together emotionally, and in a very short amount of time the two of them seemed to me like the sisters I never had. But the closest connection by far was to the one who originally didn't want to share her food or tent or bike space with me. The one who avoided work like the plague and constantly complained. The one who was more than willing to leave me to rot for dead, so she wouldn't be inconvenienced in any way: the blonde girl called Petelia.

Surprisingly we connected almost straight away, and I suddenly found myself with a new best friend who talked and laughed and bickered with me constantly. And I didn't mind one bit; I ached with loneliness in the brief time I travelled solo, not knowing where I was going or what I was doing. I was very glad for the luxury of company.

Rebel estimated that if we maintained our current speed, we'd reach Sarakonia in a few days which made me very happy. It meant my twin goals of finding Queen Elsbeth and starting a new life in a foreign land were within reach. Could I have been any luckier? I could hardly believe I was still even alive. It made me endure the scant food and water supplies and the filth and discomfort of desert life without complaint.

As the girls retired to bed that night, I sat meditating by the campfire and lost my concentration, choosing to daydream about Queen Elsbeth instead. I never bored of thinking about her, even after all those years spent wondering about her every day. In fact, it was the opposite; the more I thought about her, the more she intrigued me. I was lost in my head, enjoying my daydream when suddenly–

Yella Fella.

The familiar voice came straight into my head without any warning. I suddenly jolted and clutched at my chest.

Is that you? I asked as my heart thumped.

Jet Black, no other, he answered. *Who else do you know that can talk to you in your head?*

You're alive.

You sound disappointed.

I'm not. I'm happy for you.

Bullshit.

Did you get rescued?

Something like that.

Great. Now that we've both survived, why don't you leave me alone and go and get your own life?

That's a very sensible proposition, but what if I'm not a very sensible person?

There was an awkward pause before I broke the silence between us.

Then I think you should remember karma, I suggested.

Fuck karma and fuck you. Thought you'd be interested to know: a group of Baraktenian soldiers found me and I'm travelling with them as we speak. I'm unable to pinpoint exactly where you are right now, but when we reach Sarakonia, it'll be a very different story. I can tune into you then—

I'm not scared of you.

Really? Your heart's thumping so loud it's giving me a headache.

I'm putting the white light around me now. You won't reach—

Hold it. Before I go, remember the most important thing, the bottom line, which is this: you'll get what's coming to you and you're fucked. Have a nice evening.

I visualized a brilliant white light covering me and blocking off all communication coming from him, but it only brought small comfort, as my heart kept right on beating hard in my chest.

Elsewhere in the Desert
The Following Morning

The sea glittered peacefully in the early afternoon sun as Jet sat close to the shoreline, bare-chested and perfectly still. His travelling companions had decided to take the coastal route to Sarakonia, which was why a naked female soldier was nearby, standing waist-deep in the ocean; she was taking advantage of the afternoon travel break to wash herself.

Jet gazed at her thoughtfully. He hated the Baraktenian government and all it stood for, so theoretically he knew he was supposed to despise the soldiers. Yet in a very short space of time he'd already slept with two of them – the beautiful woman before him and a dashing, tall blonde man named Jez.

So much for political theories.

Not to worry, he reasoned. He was entitled to bend a few of his own rules if the occasion called for it. They *had* saved his life after all, and most of them were likeable people. A small few even happened to be fuckable and besides, it wasn't *appropriate* to become an enemy to them now; the timing was off.

Speaking of timing, now was the perfect moment to launch another psychic invasion. Thanks to a certain Baraktenian prick he'd recently met, he was getting quite practiced at that.

There's some past life contract between you and Queen Elsbeth that's quite intriguing Yella, he telepathed. *Do you know she's been searching for you too? She's incarnated into many bodies and travelled through many lifetimes to get to you. I see her pushing her way through in the time dimension…it's endless…she has an agenda… she searches for you tirelessly…she doesn't care how many lifetimes it takes…she's not consciously aware of this history with you of course… but the soul knows, doesn't it? The soul knows…*

His telepathic thoughts were met with silence. He tried again.

I've also tuned into your past...

Finally Yella responded. *You had no right!*

Psychics aren't readily accepted in Barakten, are they? Now if you'd been born in Sarakonia, your story would've been very different. You would've been much more accepted there. Even saluted.

It wasn't that bad.

Really? Jet scoffed. *Even your own parents turned their backs on you. Even they found you odd. They couldn't accept your gift, but don't worry, it's all behind you now, as you'll obviously never see them again.*

A hard look came into Yella's eyes. *Get out of my head,* he telepathed threateningly.

Oh dear, Jet mocked. *What have I done? Upset the apple cart? Truth's hard to swallow, isn't it? It tends to get stuck in the–*

Get out of my Goddamn head!

The words were shouted with such mental force that Jet actually obeyed. In those precious few seconds of respite, Yella visualized a white light surrounding him, permeating every cell of his body. Protecting him, growing stronger and stronger... thicker and thicker...

Jet felt the white light straight away when he tried to launch another psychic attack. He felt it pushing him back, further and further, and it pissed him off.

Get back here! he barked.

He heard the words *fuck off* so faintly in his mind he wondered if he'd imagined it.

And then there was nothing.

He tried a few more times, but the wall of white light was like a fortress now – completely impenetrable. He gritted his teeth in frustration before finally deciding to give up.

Yella was drinking morning tea with the girls at the time of the invasion and when he'd finally managed to psychically beat Jet back, it'd left him red-faced, trembling and watery-eyed. The words had cut him, as hard and as deep as a long-bladed knife through the chest.

His parents had hated both his gift and his sensitivity. They'd wanted him to carry on the family tradition – selling fish at the local markets – but being around dead fish all day did nothing but make him sick. When they learnt that he'd been indulging his true calling by giving psychic readings all hell had broken loose, and he was thrown out of the family home.

Before he'd even had a chance at reconciling with them, he'd been called on by the court officials to help find Elsbeth, and now that he was out of the country for good, he'd never see them again; guaranteed. It was too awful a fact to ruminate on, so he shut the thought out of his mind, along with his emotions.

But repressed thoughts and emotions sometimes had a habit of breaking out of their prison. Just ten minutes later, for a few dark minutes in time, he grieved deeply for his parents and dearly wished the cocky spice merchant had slowly rotted and died in the harsh desert sun, instead of being as kindly rescued as he was. He was nothing but a sadistic bastard, a dried-up dog turd, a waste of head-space. He threw his half-drunk cup to the ground and stormed off, going nowhere in particular.

"Yella!" Petelia exclaimed, staring at him oddly. "What's gotten into you?"

He ignored her and kept on walking, far too angry for a civil reply.

Elsewhere in the Desert
Ten Minutes Later

All emotion was absent, drained from consciousness as Jet floated peacefully, swaying and twirling in a wonderful mental abyss. He was in a deep meditation, with all muscles relaxed and perfectly still when suddenly his eyes flew open without warning.

"Who are you?" he asked the black bird sharply. It was standing next to him on the sand, staring at him. It said nothing. He tried again. "Don't pretend you don't hear or understand me sir, when I know you do. You've been following us around for days and I'm getting tired of it. State your business and be done with it. What is it that you want?"

The bird suddenly shape-shifted into a fully grown, bearded man wearing a long black robe. He grinned and tipped his head in greeting. "Very good, I'm impressed. How did you know it was me?"

Jet didn't even flinch; he was no virgin to sorcery. "I'm a psychic; I can pick up on energy, sir. And yours wasn't that of a dumb animal."

"*That*, my friend, is very debatable."

Jet smiled. "Your presence is nothing short of extraordinary. It pervades the space around you. It pervades *me*. It's a force so powerful I can barely even begin to describe it."

Steele laughed. "That's right. The great power of sorcery… given to a man such as myself…it should be a criminal offense. But I'll take that as a compliment anyway."

"It was meant that way," Jet replied, watching him closely.

"Enough about me. I'm curious about *you*. I see you travelling with the soldiers, but you have no uniform."

"The name's Jet." He smiled as he stood up and offered his hand. "I'm a spice merchant from Sarakonia, and it's a complete honor to meet you."

The two men shook hands firmly.

"Were you robbed?"

"Something like that," Jet nodded. "I see you have a good knowledge of the hazards of desert life."

Steele shrugged. "And so I should. I've been living in it for over a hundred years now."

"You still haven't answered my question about what you want," Jet reminded him.

"Who is she?" Steele asked, indicating the naked woman washing herself in the sea. She was out of earshot with her back turned to them, completely unaware that two men in the distance were now staring at and talking about her.

"So *that's* what this has been all about? You've been following us because of her?"

"She's very pretty." *How very wrong*, he suddenly thought. *'Pretty' is an understatement. 'Pretty' is beneath her.*

The woman was so much more than 'pretty'; she was drop-dead gorgeous, and he'd lost count of the number of times he'd turned himself into bird form, sitting on a tree trunk or pretending to pick at something on the ground, just for the privilege of being near her, of eavesdropping in on her conversations.

She had reminded him of an ex-lover he'd had around a hundred years back. Physically she was mesmerizing, with long, thick, dark hair, brown eyes and generous breasts; he'd checked when she was bathing a couple of times, just to make sure.

"That she is," Jet agreed. "Do you want her? Perhaps we can make a wager."

"What are you saying?"

"I gather you can teleport people as a sorcerer?"

He shrugged. "Of course."

"I'm looking for a Baraktenian man; tall, pale and blue eyed, with brown short hair. Looks to be in his early twenties. He's a psychic that answers to the name of Yella Fella, and he's somewhere in this desert as we speak. If you bring him to me, I promise she's yours to do as you please."

Steele regarded him thoughtfully. "Why are you offering this?"

"The soldiers need his help to find Queen Elsbeth of Barakten, as she's been abducted and apparently imprisoned in Sarakonia," he replied. "They're going there to get her back, but in a country with a population of around three million, finding her isn't going to be a simple task. I promise you; they'll be more than happy to give you the services of the girl in exchange for your services of giving them the psychic. It's nothing to them, as they need to find their Queen, no matter what the cost."

"The deal is off," Steele said irritably, slashing a hand through the air. "I'm well aware of this 'Queen' you speak of, and she is a nothing but a whore. I refuse to play any part whatsoever in her rescue."

"She had extreme policies and as a result of that, was unpopular with many people," Jet conceded. "Myself included. But you needn't concern yourself with her anymore. The chances of finding her alive were always going to be next to nil and besides, I strongly feel she's dead already. Trust me. You've already seen my psychic abilities, haven't you?"

"Satisfy my curiosity. What do they need *him* for, when they can just use your psychic abilities for information?"

"The Baraktenians are a conservative people and normally psychics don't get much respect from them. Yella's unique though; he has a long track record of successfully locating dead bodies and missing persons, which means they trust him. His word would definitely be favored over an unknown psychic like me."

"What's in this for you?" Steele asked suspiciously. "And how do I know they'll keep their end of the bargain if I do such a thing?"

Jet didn't miss a beat. "These soldiers have saved my life. I owe them a great debt, and the fact of the matter is, the sooner they find her, dead *or* alive, the faster they can get back to their homeland and get on with their lives. As for keeping their end of the bargain, what sort of fool would even *think* of deceiving a sorcerer as powerful as yourself, someone that could kill any one of them in the blink of an eye if he so chose?"

He paused, waiting for Steele to respond but he said nothing, looking to be in deep thought.

Finally, Steele spoke. "This psychic man is in the desert as we speak?"

"Yes."

"Merchants are the only ones permitted to leave Barakten, so I gather he's escaped the country illegally."

"Yes."

"Then he would be severely punished, possibly even killed by the soldiers for his disobedience, would he not?"

"Maybe. Maybe not. Will you not at least consider the offer sir? Having already tasted the goods, I can thoroughly recommend this woman, sexually speaking. Trust me, she's very, shall we say, *responsive*." He winked meaningfully. "She wouldn't disappoint."

"Believe it or not sir, that's not all I'm after."

"Oh?"

"She reminds me of someone I once knew. A former girlfriend, in fact."

"Then it would be all the more pleasing to have her then, wouldn't it?" Jet reasoned.

"This is beginning to sound interesting," the sorcerer mused. "Allow me to think about it."

"More to the point, think about *her*," Jet encouraged. "All ripe for the taking. Her name's Klo, by the way. Be assured, I'll tell the soldiers who you are and what you can do for them."

Steele looked thoughtful for a few more seconds, then suddenly shape-shifted into a crow before swiftly taking off towards the sea, purposely coming to a stop in front of Klo's perfect form in the water. He flapped on the spot only a meter away from her, at head level. Horrified, she covered her breasts and screamed.

Come now, madam! Steele thought. *Surely I'm not that ugly?*

She tried splashing sea water at the bird, hoping to frighten it away, but it didn't work in the slightest. It stayed exactly where it was for at least a full minute, flapping its wings as it drank in every inch of her delectable nakedness.

Klo was totally confused as to why the bird was staring at her so intensely. What the hell did it want? Was it going to attack? She decided to dive underwater to escape its attention – giving Steele a great view of her naked ass – and when she finally came to the surface for some well-needed air, it was nowhere to be seen.

 ~

Two Days Later, Morning
Yella Speaks

So far the three of us had been managing well, despite the discomforts and the meagre food supply, but that morning I woke up with a creepy feeling of dread. Death was crawling through my mind, and I had a sick feeling that our luck was about to run out that day; that at some point our lives would hang in the balance; that at least one of us would be dead before nightfall.

Unfortunately there wasn't a lot I could do about my premonition except suffer it, hope it was just paranoia, and pray that the day would be over with as fast as possible. I tried to distract myself with other thoughts.

After the last encounter with the spice merchant, I made sure I was never without the white light. I surrounded myself with it day and night and forced myself not to think of him, as it was the same as thinking of the pits of hell. I tried to imagine putting him in a cupboard in the back of my mind and locking it.

He wouldn't taunt me with his sick thoughts ever again, as I'd no longer allow him anywhere near me psychically. But he still lived and breathed in that cupboard, and I knew he'd try his hardest to break free, and maybe one day he would. And then we'd meet again. I feared that day, and I feared him, and the trouble was he knew it and fed on it like a miserable desert vulture.

I hoped to forget him, but it wasn't easy. He was at least as psychically gifted as I was, and just as capable of finding Elsbeth in Sarakonia. I prayed that I'd be the one to get to her first, for if he laid a finger on that precious body of hers, I'd have to kill him, and then I'd be a murderer. And then how would I cope with being a murderer?

Elsbeth was always in my thoughts. Always. I fantasized about her at dawn, only it felt so real I had to smile. This is how it went: Elsbeth and I are husband and wife in Sarakonia, with two lovely children, a comfortable home, and a sprawling garden. I come home to her after a day of psychic reading at the markets and after spending a pleasant evening with our children, we put them to bed and then make love. I think of our bodies lovingly wrapped around each other; of sweet, deep kisses and soft, pale skin. And a number other things. At that point in the fantasy, I started breathing heavily in between Petelia and Rebel in the tent and it felt a bit odd, so I went outside, walked a fair distance, and finally relieved my poor aching cock.

An hour later we were ordered by Rebel to gather root vegetables and water, as she'd decided we needed to stock up on supplies before we did any more travelling. Meanwhile she took off alone on the bike hunting for wild desert pig, although where she'd find them, I wouldn't know. Being vegetarian, I wasn't looking forward to the sickening smell of cooking meat but there wasn't a lot I could do about it, as both Rebel and Petelia were big meat-eaters.

Rebel had taught me that despite looking incredibly barren, food and water were plentiful and abounded everywhere in the desert. I learned which type of desert bush harbored the root vegetables we sustained ourselves with, and which type of cactus contained drinkable water. We'd slash at the cactus with our knives and our water pouches would catch the life-giving water that seethed from its trunk. We dug up the root vegetables, stashing them away in our supply bags. I was glad to finally be useful; I even enjoyed helping with setting up the tent and cooking.

I was going about my business, routinely trying to draw water, when I accidentally cut my finger on a sharp prickle of a cactus, drawing blood; I took that as a very bad sign. More ominous feelings came (for no reason whatsoever) as Petelia walked towards me, supply bag in hand, taking a break from her morning chores for a sociable chat. She was firmly convinced that Rebel didn't really like her, and wouldn't be persuaded otherwise.

"I don't understand how you could say that," I said. "Weren't the three of us talking and laughing for hours last night? What was that? The actions of someone that supposedly hates you?"

"We had a big argument before you came along where she turned on me, all screams and threats," she confided. "I honestly thought she was going to kill me. It's not funny," she said irritably when she saw the amused look on my face. "I was really scared. I honestly thought that she might fly off the handle and get violent. Or even worse; take off and leave, and imagine what would happen to me after that?"

"You'd join a sand monster tribe?" I smirked. "As an honorary member?"

"You are incorrigible, mister Yella Fella." She swatted my shoulder.

"Don't worry, you'll adjust to one another; it's just a matter of time. Now I'd better get back to my chores before she threatens to kill me as well," I joked.

She stopped me with a hand on my arm and an anxious look. "Do you think we'll be alright?" She looked into my eyes intently. "Seriously. Do you think we'll survive this? I've heard some pretty awful stories from Rebel. They really worry me."

"Absolutely," I replied, with much more confidence than I felt. "We're doing well so far, aren't we?"

"Just promise me one thing. No matter what happens."

"Which is?"

"Don't leave me. I'm not good at being alone."

"How could I possibly leave one so beautiful?" I smiled.

She smiled back. "I always feel so comfortable with you."

"That's sweet of you to say," I said, feeling my cheeks flush. "I also feel very comfortable with you."

"I can barely stand it here anymore," she said, suddenly shifting back to whining mode again. "I'm not capable like you and Rebel are. I was brought up very differently."

That part was definitely right; she was the laziest, most incapable person I'd ever met, but it didn't seem very gentlemanly to say so.

"Come on," I soothed. "You know that's not true."

"It *is* true," she argued. "I'm so useless I may as well be a stick person. I can't hunt, I can't set up a tent, I can't start a fire, and I can't cook. I've never learned how to. I can't even boil stupid water properly."

"You're being way too hard on yourself."

"How can you say that when all I do is complain all the time, on top of cooking like crap?"

"You really *are* in a mood today, aren't you? Things could always be worse."

She gave me a cynical look. "How could things possibly be any–"

A howl came from the desert, cutting off whatever else she'd been about to say. It sounded faint, from a fair distance, but it made all the hairs on my arms stand up on end and my heart suddenly fill with terror. It sounded like the howl of a wolf, but I knew it was no wolf; it was a sand monster, a creature I prayed I'd never meet in the desert. Petelia and I stared at each other in horror for a few seconds, temporarily lost for words.

"We should run," I said seriously, taking her hand.

We hastily dropped our supplies and ran till our limbs ached with exhaustion, trying to get away from where the howls were coming from. But the sounds, instead of fading, seemed only to be getting louder, more urgent, and more numerous, though we still couldn't see anything. Petelia, unused to strenuous physical activity, soon started to tire and I half-led, half-dragged her along the desert plain.

Suddenly she screamed, "Oh God! Yella! I see creatures!"

"Where?" I gasped, and we stopped with a jolt.

"Over there!" She pointed a finger to the right. I saw a cluster of brown figures sprinting towards us in the far distance. We high-tailed it to the left. I had a vague plan of reaching the small hill in front of us and hiding somewhere. Anywhere. It was around a hundred meters away and was our only hope. We couldn't keep running forever; we were dealing with wild creatures who were much bigger and stronger than us.

Then things went from bad to worse: Petelia collapsed with exhaustion, and I had to carry her over my shoulder while running at the same time. In my peripheral vision I saw several creatures shoot up from the ground like rockets all around us, some just fifty meters away, their speed and power evident in their lightning-fast strides.

Then I tripped over a rock, and it was the final nail in the coffin. We both fell in a disorderly heap on the sandy ground and before we could even get up, we were surrounded by sand dust and brown giants. Petelia and I coughed and squinted at them through the dust as we clung to each other in terror. They almost looked human, with their powerful muscles and satisfied expressions. They stood rooted to the ground amidst the sand dust for a few seconds, regarding us curiously, then we saw their long, sharp claws and bared fangs as they slowly came toward us. We both screamed.

Suddenly the ear-splitting sound of continuous gunshots punctured the air. Petelia and I shut our eyes, lay on the ground and clung to each other like limpets. More sand was flung into the air as giant bodies either crashed to the ground after being struck or dived down into the earth for refuge. Then suddenly the bullets stopped.

"Get the fuck on! Hurry!"

It was Rebel, sitting on her bike and screaming at us. We sprinted towards her, keeping our heads low while dodging the giant bodies lying on the ground, writhing and howling loudly in pain.

Once we were both safely on the bike, Rebel rode at top speed as the engine roared loudly through the desert air. She was finally able to fully concentrate on the path in front of her, and she swerved and weaved expertly around endless bushes and rocks with one hand on the handlebar and the other on her machine gun. Petelia clung tightly to me as I gritted my teeth in terror, our filthy hair dancing madly in the wind. I couldn't help but look behind me, ever alert for deadly sprinting monsters with razor-sharp claws and teeth.

I wasn't sure how much time had passed as we drove through the desert. I was only just starting to recover from the near-miss of being ripped apart by giant sand monsters when Rebel suddenly stopped the bike, parked, and packed the machine gun she'd been carrying safely away in the supply bag at the side of the bike. While she was there, she got out some water bottles and ordered us to drink.

"Take a big gulp," she said. "It could be several hours before you get to drink again."

"I don't understand," Petelia said, looking worried.

"There's a strong chance there could be a sandstorm," she explained. "The wind's picking up."

She then threw what she called 'face masks' at us (which were very efficient Baraktenian army equipment specially made for sandstorms) and ordered us to put them on, demonstrating how to do so. It was an ugly-looking thing that completely covered the face and neck and contained a breathing apparatus and goggles.

Apparently we needed those face masks. Sand could get in your eyes and blind you, Rebel explained, or get in your lungs and suffocate you. Also, sand travelling at sixty miles an hour or more tends to hurt a bit, she said, so should there be a storm, make sure all your body parts are covered up.

"Say a storm does hit," I said as we started putting on the masks. "Could we possibly outrun it?"

"Well I'll try, so if it happens, hold on tight," Rebel answered.

"What if we can't outrun it?" Petelia asked anxiously.

"Then we're fucked," she replied without any emotion, before putting on her mask and getting back on the bike.

The crappy day continued on being crappy – just thirty minutes later, there was a full-blown sandstorm, despite my mental praying, pleading and begging for there *not* to be one. And it wasn't just a small, insignificant or even mediocre sandstorm; oh no. True to the awful day it was, it was a powerful brownish-orange mega-force that engulfed us completely. A force that easily tore us away from both the bike and each other. A force that swept me through the air like a small rag doll and thudded me to the ground and rolled me downhill.

Suddenly there was nothing in my world but a violent mess of loud howling winds, jagged movement, flying rocks and walls of sand, and my own helplessly flailing arms and legs. Mercifully my fall was eventually cushioned by a desert bush that happened to be in my way, and I spent the rest of the storm clinging to it while the winds raged wildly around me. It was impossible to see or get to my friends in the brownish-orange haze and I was terrified for them, but I couldn't do a thing. All I could do was endure the battering storm, cover myself as best as I could, and pray for their lives.

Elsewhere in the Desert

A storm is coming, Steele thought.

He was in crow form, hundreds of feet above the Baraktenian Desert's surface, flying at great speed through clouds that were beginning to grey.

And not just any storm. This one is a big one, I can feel it. Where is Jet, the soldiers and Klo?

He started lowering himself towards the ground, carefully scanning the desert's surface as he did so. Anybody else would look at its grounds and think everything was the same. Not him. He could land anywhere and know exactly where he was. He knew every bush, every hill and every rock as well as his own bird claws; that's what living as a half-bird, half-man for centuries did to you.

Being a powerful sorcerer also afforded him many luxuries: he could dematerialize and shape-shift at will, without leaving a trace, which meant he could live his different lives in peace, with not a soul to check up on him.

Over the centuries he'd single-handedly saved countless lives in the Baraktenian Desert, until eventually coming up with the idea of establishing a hospital there to help the sick and injured. Setting up a hospital in the desert was far more practical than teleporting sick people to the overcrowded hospitals in Sarakonia, which he used to do all the time.

It took a good ten minutes of flying to spot the squadron he'd been stalking – he found them heading north in their very recognizable black uniforms, with one psychic hanger-on.

He lowered himself even closer to the ground. Down. Down. Down. He was flying fast, swooping in at shoulder height from behind them.

Jet was traveling as a passenger on the back of a motorbike at the time, feeling a little stiff from hours on end of sitting when he saw a large black bird, the size of an eagle, only meters away to his right. He eyed it suspiciously. Could it be who he thought it was? He turned his eyes from it for only a few seconds and when he looked for it again, it'd vanished, as though it'd been nothing but an illusion.

Sorcery, he thought knowingly. Steele obviously hadn't forgotten about him or the soldiers. What was he doing here, he wondered? What did he want? Was he just routinely obsessing over Klo, or was something else going on?

When the squadron reached a hill crest, they saw a dark-haired man standing in the distance on flat ground, holding his hands up for them to stop. He stood in complete isolation, with no tent, bike, supplies, carry animal or other person in sight, which made for a very strange sight in the desert wilderness. He deliberately waited until the very last bike had stopped in front of him before he spoke and got straight to the point, not even bothering to introduce himself. His expression was serious, his voice deep and strong as he spoke.

"A great storm is coming. You must follow me if you are to survive it. I know this desert very well; there is a cave where you can take shelter till it's over."

The soldiers formed a tight circle around him and watched him closely, in case he went ape-shit and decided to pull a gun, but he didn't show an ounce of nervousness or fear in their presence. On the contrary, there was great confidence and authority in the strange, dark-haired man's voice, as if he expected them all to believe and obey him without question. As if he were some sort of God, used to being obeyed.

Various members of the squadron looked at each other in confusion, then all eyes fell to their leader, Rixx, to respond.

Rixx, a stocky, broad-shouldered man with close-cropped brown hair, responded by getting his gun out of its holster and pointing it straight at him.

"Who the fuck are you?" he asked, getting straight to the point. "Where do you come from and whaddaya want? Where are your transport and supplies?"

"I'm a sorcerer, and my name is Steele Silver. I come from everywhere and nowhere, and I don't need transport or supplies," he answered irritably. "There's a good chance you will all *die* if you don't do as I say, do you understand? The storm that's coming is not just any storm. It's a big one, not seen for many years."

"He speaks the truth," Jet said, and then suddenly all eyes were on the spice merchant. "We're in the presence of a great power and believe me, we'd all be fools not to do as he says."

Rixx was far from impressed. "I've heard of sorcerers for years, and I think it's all bullshit," he said casually. "I've never believed in 'em, which means I've just decided I don't like you very much."

"You might not believe in us sir, but we are everywhere," Steele replied. "In this desert, in Sarakonia, even in Barakten, where you come–"

"Bullshit," Rixx interrupted. "You're either insane, or this is a trick. You could be in with them half-man half-pigs out there who all want us dead, so I think you should fuck off right now before I shoot you."

"How *dare* you talk to me like that!"

"Yeah, how *dare* I talk to you like that," Rixx echoed. "Some ugly mother-fucker liar who just sprang out of nowhere, giving us orders."

"I'm not a liar, nor am I ugly," Steele replied, feeling his voice rising. "Do you want me to prove myself to you sir? I can do that right here, right now if you–"

"Don't prove anything 'cause I'm not interested," Rixx interrupted again. "And just for the record," he said, leaning forward and looking him straight in the eyes for extra emphasis, "you're as ugly as a desert pig's ass."

Laughter swept throughout the group as Steele's expression darkened.

"Now I thought I just told you to go." Rixx waved his gun dismissively, as if he were shooing an annoying fly away.

Steele walked towards Rixx, his stride strong and purposeful. "I'm as ugly as a desert pig's ass?" he repeated, his tone dangerous. "Excuse me? Is that what my ears are telling me?"

Jet, closely observing the scene, had a panicked look on his face and was just about to say something when–

"Stop or I'll shoot, motherfucker!" Rixx shouted, his face reddening. Steele ignored him and kept on walking, so he fired. To his and everyone else's horror, the bullets just bounced off the dark-haired stranger's body, as if he wasn't human, but something else. What else Rixx didn't know, but he was coming towards him like he meant violence and the bullets weren't stopping him.

What the fuck? he thought.

Seconds later, another hail of bullets descended on Steele's body as the squadron, fiercely protecting their leader, fired their guns, but their bullets too were just bouncing off and dropping to the ground around him. Jet hurried off his bike and kept screaming "Hold your fire! Hold your fire!" like a wild mantra, but no-one was listening in the mayhem.

The sorcerer reached Rixx in no time at all and soon the squadron leader was up in the air, his big feet kicking out desperately. His entire body weight was being held up by a single hand and his neck was being squeezed with incredibly strong force.

Jet came as close to Steele as he dared in the gunfire, still screaming at the squadron to stop and holding his hands up.

When they finally ceased firing, he looked up at Rixx and saw the color of his face change. A cacophony of screams and shouting sounded around him. The soldiers were all on their feet now, having gotten off their bikes, and quickly formed a rough circle around the sorcerer.

"Put him down! Put him down!" Jet pleaded desperately. He was shouting, looking quickly from Steele to Rixx, his heart pounding rapidly in his chest. "You're killing him!"

"I believe that's the general idea," Steele replied casually, and kept on squeezing.

Jet's mind raced. "He was just doing as soldiers do!" he said quickly. "They're trained not to trust anyone! They know nothing of magic, or sorcerers, or tact! They only know how to fight!"

"You were supposed to tell them about me, remember?" he said as he squeezed, not taking his eyes off Rixx for a second. "As we agreed?"

"I didn't get a chance! We only spoke yesterday!"

"Not very organized, are you?"

Please!" Jet begged. "For the love of God! Let the man go! You'll kill him!"

"Too late," Steele replied neutrally, dropping the leader's sizeable body to the ground with a thud. "He's already dead."

Collective gasps and screams filled the air as Jet lowered his head and ran his fingers through his hair, deliberately turning away from the distasteful sight of the corpse. This was a very stressful situation – he needed time to think, and there was none. Everyone was in fucking hysterics; a bunch of brawny hot-heads with an even more powerful hot-head. He had to do or say something fast, before they all started fucking killing one another – and even worse, included *him* in the death tally.

Jet's lover, the tall blond soldier named Jez, charged towards Steele like a wild animal. "I'm gonna kill you, motherfucker!"

he screamed. "I'm gonna kill you!" Two male soldiers strained to hold him back as he struggled to break their grip.

"No Jez, no!" Jet warned, holding his hands up. "You don't stand a chance!"

A few soldiers, including Klo, knelt by their beloved leader's body, stroking him and sobbing broken-heartedly.

"These people are the biggest fools I've ever seen," Steele told Jet as he walked towards him amongst the ruckus. "I may as well be a brick wall, as they will not listen to a single word I say. I think I might take just Klo and yourself to the cave for shelter and be done with it. The rest of these idiots can die, and good riddance. I'm done I tell you. I've had it."

"Don't leave them to die," Jet said, desperately begging again. "Please. I keep telling you, they're soldiers who know nothing of magic or sorcery. They're practical people, not like you or me. Just let me talk to them."

"Fine," Steele replied, eyeing the soldier who charged at him sulkily. "You have five minutes."

Jet took a deep breath, steeled himself to remain calm, and faced the large group of angry soldiers square on. "Listen to me, all of you!" he shouted. "I'm as sorry about Rixx as you are, but this man is speaking the truth! If you don't follow him to shelter, there's a strong chance you won't survive the impending–"

"Save us the lecture, professor," a stocky female soldier with a buzz cut snarled. "Where's the fuckin' proof of a storm? I don't see nuthin'."

"Look behind you," Jet replied evenly. "Great dust clouds are visible in the distance as we speak."

Collective heads turned and saw the evidence for themselves.

"Fall out! We're following him," a soldier ordered roughly. He was taller and thinner than Rixx had been and immediately assumed leadership of the squadron.

"But whadda we do about Rixx?" Klo objected, tears streaming down her cheeks. "We can't just leave him here!"

"You deaf?" the new leader barked, jogging to his bike. "I *said*, fall out!"

Klo glared at him. "Fuck you!" She was horrified at Rixx's death, but years of survival training was firmly embedded in her psyche. She took a final, anguished look at the lifeless face of her beloved former leader – a man who'd been a father figure to her for many years – then jogged to her bike to leave like everyone else.

Jez saw Steele shape-shift into a bird and seized the opportunity to throw a large rock at him with all the strength he had. It wasn't a bad throw, but frustratingly he missed his mark, as the great black bird was already way ahead of the group, concentrating on leading them to shelter. Cursing furiously and with adrenalin pumping through him, he sprinted to his bike and drove at top speed as he followed the others.

Maybe I'll get lucky. Land a gunshot on the feathered fuck, he thought.

He thought grimly of Rixx being eaten by a vulture or sand monster; it was inevitable in the desert. He gritted his teeth and grunted savagely, solidly punching the silver handlebar on his bike a couple of times, barely registering that in the process he'd drawn blood, and it was trickling wetly around his fingers. Surviving the storm was the last thing on this mind; all he could think of was ripping the crow (or sorcerer or freak or whatever the fuck he was) apart with his bare hands for what he'd just done to Rixx.

Ten Minutes Later

Two curious soldiers viewed the sandstorm through the vantage point of a small crack. Despite faint sounds of howling winds in the distance, silence pervaded as the rest of the squadron sat glumly around the cave, their torches illuminating the darkness.

There was nothing to do but wait, but the waiting felt like a slow form of torture, like listening to the constant drip of a leaky tap, mixed in with terrible feelings of anger, sadness, and devastation.

⤙∼⤚

Three Hours Later
Elsewhere in the Desert
Yella Speaks

After the storm I'd ripped my restrictive, claustrophobic mask off and tossed it away. Bruised and battered, with sand-filled, matted hair sticking out everywhere, I stumbled around the desert like a zombie, in an almost trance-like daze.

Till I saw something that quickly snapped me out of it.

A dark-haired head stuck out from the sand in the distance, about five meters to my right; adrenalin instantly kicked in and I ran like hell.

"Rebel!" I yelled. "Oh God! Rebel!"

She was buried from the chin down and looked unconscious, her head tilted lifelessly to the side. *She's not dead,* I prayed, digging like a mad man to get her out of her sandy grave, clawing at the ground with my hands. Then I remembered the knife in my pocket, shakily retrieved it, and stabbed at the earth with all my strength.

I didn't let myself even *think* of the possibility that she might be dead. My only thought was to dig her out as fast as I could, so I just kept on digging my guts out when a dark-haired man suddenly appeared out of nowhere, squatting alongside me.

"Looks like you need some help," he said calmly, chewing on gum.

I looked at him oddly for a few seconds, noting dark hair, beard and yellow eyes, before returning to my mad digging. "Help me get her out, help me get her out," I said breathlessly.

He laughed shortly. "You're in the best of hands. I'll do all that and more, my friend."

But still he squatted next to me, watching me work and doing nothing.

"Help me, whoever you are!" I exploded. "Don't just squat around looking at me! She could die!"

He shrugged. "As you wish, but I do believe she's already–"

A gigantic and incredibly muscular sand monster suddenly shot out of the ground at waist level, spraying sand all over the three of us. I screamed as I dropped the knife, falling heavily on my ass as I desperately crawled backwards to get away from it. It was only meters away as it roared, the strong guttural sound echoing through to the core of my bones. Baring sharp yellowish fangs, it leisurely started to pull the rest of its body up from the ground.

The dark-haired man didn't even bother getting up, and calmly spat out the gum in his mouth. "Piss off!" he shouted irritably, as if he was swatting a big fly. It took one look at him and dived back into the ground again, sinking into the earth as easily as a river, spraying sand in my hair and mouth again as it disappeared.

I'll never forget what happened next: one moment I was sitting on the desert earth, panting and trembling and spitting out sand, and the next I was sitting on a white stone floor. I was no longer in a harsh and unforgiving desert with a man-eating sand monster, and Rebel wasn't buried up to her neck in the ground anymore. She was in the arms of the dark-haired man, and he was standing in a corridor of a great white-stone mansion supported by giant columns, a place as calm and as peaceful as a heavenly monastery. I looked around me in shock and awe, thinking of the possibility of being just a character in a vivid dream.

"Don't worry," he soothed. "There are no sand monsters in this building. It's protected by magic. You are very safe here."

"Where am I?"

"Still in the Baraktenian Desert but in a hospital," he answered in a business-like tone. "I set this up many years ago for sick and injured stragglers. Come along now," he ordered. "Get up and walk with me." He started down the corridor.

I sprang up as I followed him, heart still racing from my recent brush with death. "Who are you?"

"I'm a sorcerer," he answered. "And may I say that you and your friend are very, very lucky I came along when I did."

"I've heard of sorcerers all my life. All my life. Without ever fully believing in them."

"Well, you may be forced to revise that theory."

"Will she be alright?" I asked anxiously.

"She's as dead as a doornail," he answered. "However," he added, seeing the look of alarm on my face, "I can bring her back to life. Are there any more of you left in the desert, by the way?"

"Yes," I replied. "A blonde woman, twenty-one-years-old, and–"

"I'll get her later," he interrupted dismissively. "She shouldn't be too far from where I found you."

I looked around, noting that the entire building was mostly made of white stone. The ceiling was very high and there were several large, clear glass windows on the right-hand side and rooms with wooden doors on the left. Several paintings of naked women decorated the walls and a few large ferns in giant white ceramic pots dotted the corridor's floor.

I was still bewildered, disorientated and firmly locked in survival mode. I really hoped that what I was seeing and hearing was the truth, and that I wasn't still in the desert somewhere, going mad and hallucinating.

"Do you like the place?" he asked casually, and without waiting for a response said, "It's got everything: food, water, entertainment, bedding, baths. It's even got a pool," he boasted. "I designed it myself. It's got nurses too; you'll be seeing them shortly."

We entered a large bedroom. I saw a king-sized bed, with silken blue sheets and a blue, ornately designed bedspread. A glass window revealed the peaceful desert landscape outside. A single wooden chair and two small wooden tables stood alongside the bed, one of them holding a large jug of water, cup, large spoon and neatly folded blue towel. The wooden chest on the other side held a folded blue face cloth and a generous fruit bowl.

As he carefully laid Rebel down on the massive bed, I immediately reached over and felt for her neck. "There's no pulse," I said with rising hysteria. "There's no pulse!"

"She's *dead*, lad. I've already told you," he replied bluntly.

That statement was the culmination of what had been a very, very, very bad day. My head dropped as the awful words finally sank their way into my exhausted brain, and I sat on the edge of the bed, crying like a baby. I must have looked pathetic, like a big girl, but the emotions inside were like a tornado, forcing their way out of me whether I liked it or not. She'd been a good friend to me, I'd really liked her, and her death hurt, as if it punched me hard in the face before ripping my heart out of my chest. She'd been young too, just in her twenties. The sorcerer watched me thoughtfully for a few seconds, then clamped a hand down on my shoulder as he sat alongside me.

"I understand you're in shock," he said firmly. "I also understand this is all very new and strange to you, that you're definitely not used to someone like me. But your friend *will* wake up tomorrow morning alive, I promise you. My magic is, shall we say, far too complex to explain in a way that you can quickly understand, and I don't think you're in a fit state to take much in anyway, so for now can you just try to relax and trust that what I'm saying is the truth?"

I looked at him with tears streaming down my cheeks. There was nothing much to say, so I just nodded. He smiled at me, and his bright yellow eyes seemed to soften.

"Good lad," he said, slapping me on the back. "Now come along. Get up and shut the door behind you. A nurse will attend to the woman, but for now she needs to be left alone."

Chapter Four

Elsewhere in the Desert

Petelia took her time getting up after the storm had eventually died down, slowly and carefully uncurling herself from the tight ball she'd deliberately wrapped herself into. Everything was stiff and hurt like hell; most notably her right side, where the wind had mercilessly thrown her against the ground and she'd rolled continuously, like a demented ball. It had been the most frightening experience of her life, that feeling of being completely helpless and out of control, of being so easily torn apart from both the bike and her friends. She thought she might've sprained her ankle too; it throbbed painfully, but she knew she had to get up and walk if there was any chance at all of surviving. On top of everything else, she was dying of thirst and her tongue felt like it was covered in fur.

Where the fuck are the others and how dare they leave me like this? she thought angrily as she slowly limped her way up the hill, pushing her dirty, matted hair out of the way. Her body was not in a good state, but it could've been far, far worse, she reasoned. At least she'd come to this desert well prepared, with sensible, sturdy footwear, a shirt with long sleeves, and trousers.

She took her mask off and threw it away. She figured she wouldn't need it anymore and besides, it was annoying and uncomfortable.

She took a good look around for the first time and whimpered softly at what she saw: endless clumps of grass, bush, rock, sand, and rolling hills, with not a single human in sight. Not. One. Damn. Single. Human.

Not even Rebel either.

Crap!

Her heart sunk down all the way to her knees, and her whimpering increased a little, but she pressed on regardless, swollen ankle and all. She'd barely gone ten steps when a sound she remembered all too well stopped her in her tracks; a sound that sent sharp spikes of terror echoing through to the core of her very being: a drawn out, soul-haunting howl.

⌁

Desert Hospital
Yella Speaks

The corridor spilled into a large lounge/dining room area. Sweet Lord! The sorcerer seemed totally obsessed with the female form, as everywhere I turned the walls were generously decorated with images of mostly naked women. A large, two-meter high white marble statue of a naked woman stood proudly in the center of the room, seemingly proudly showing off her assets. On one side there was an assortment of giant cushions on the floor, and on the other a kitchen with a long wooden table and chairs nearby.

I finally discovered that the sorcerer's name was Steele. He'd been feeding and watering me for the last half hour as we sat at the kitchen table talking. I'd calmed down a lot, but the tension was soon climbing up yet again, as he didn't seem in any hurry to rescue Petelia. In fact, he'd snapped at me earlier when I'd tried to bring the subject up again.

"Satisfy my curiosity and tell me who the three of you are and what you were doing," he ordered, looking relaxed as he held a large glass of red wine in his hand.

I didn't feel the need to lie to protect myself. I'd heard sorcerers had no allegiances with any man-made kingdoms or laws; with their powers they were a law unto themselves. So I told him the truth. "We sought to escape and start our lives over in Sarakonia. Rebel, the one you rescued, is an ex-soldier who deserted the army. The other one sought to escape a husband who beat her."

"How interesting," he said, playing with his chin thoughtfully. "What is your name?"

"Yella Fella."

He raised his eyebrows at that and there was a long, awkward pause before he finally spoke again. "I see. And the blonde girl's name?"

"Petelia." I paused and took a breath. "Speaking of which, do you mind getting her now? Please," I begged. "I'm very worried."

"I've already told you that I would get her later and that I wish to talk to you first," he reminded me.

"She could be dead by then," I pointed out.

"Don't be ridiculous," he scoffed.

"What's ridiculous about that?"

"Don't argue with me," he snapped. His gaze was suddenly so fierce he nearly burnt a hole through me. "I *said*," he emphasized, "that I would get her later. Just be patient, will you?"

At that point, with growing alarm, I started wondering if I was dealing with a man who was both powerful and dangerous; both mighty and insane.

Elsewhere in the Desert

One howl turned to several. Some sounded close, some further away. The howls pounded in Petelia's head, and all pain and discomfort in her body was instantly forgotten as adrenalin surged through her, pushing her forward, even as she trembled, limped, and whimpered like a baby. She couldn't bring herself to turn to look at them; her instincts were telling her not to. Her instincts were telling her to move, and to keep on moving, as fast as she could go.

Desert Hospital
Yella Speaks

We were still talking, and I was still tense. I took a big gulp of water from the glass in my hand.

"Tell me more about yourself. I'm curious as to why you escaped Barakten," he said conversationally as he sipped his red wine.

"Queen Elsbeth II was recently abducted from her bedroom chambers," I replied. "I'm known as a psychic, so I was called on by the court officials to help find her. I gave them information but they wanted more, and I really tried but I couldn't give them exactly what they wanted. I was in fear for my life, so I escaped."

"She's dead," he said bluntly. "I've heard it from a reliable source."

I shook my head, taking another gulp of water. "There've been many rumors, but I feel she's alive. And I don't believe she's as evil as people say either."

He stared at me as his fingers tapped slowly on the table, brow rising, and my palms instantly started sweating.

"She cast out thousands of innocent citizens from their own country," he said. "Thousands. How can she *not* be evil?"

"I feel that a man's behind her, possibly even a sorcerer. He's been forcing her to pull strings that she doesn't want to move, but she's got no choice. She must do what he says, as he's the one with the real power, not her, but at this point I can't identify who he is."

"You are sorely misguided, my friend. The Baraktenians were banished from their homeland by her orders alone," he said.

"Many people believe that," I replied. "But belief and truth aren't always a match."

The sorcerer smashed his wine glass to the ground and let me know exactly what he thought of my theories. "Don't give me your idiotic lectures about the truth! The truth is very simple!" he barked, waving his hands around theatrically. "Everything was her fault! Everything! She didn't want what she classified as second-class citizens hanging around and soiling her precious country! There it is, my so-called psychic, and there is nothing complicated about it! Are we going to keep on arguing like this? Because it's starting to put me in a foul mood." He glared at me with his strange yellow eyes. "Do you have any idea how *dangerous* that is?"

Elsewhere in the Desert

There was no way to tell exactly how close or far away they were from the howls; only that they seemed to be talking to each other in their animal language, telling each other where she was. Oh God, the howling was increasing and getting louder, as if they were in a frenzy!

"Help!" Petelia screamed to the desert skies, heart pounding fiercely in her chest. "Help!"

~~~

Desert Hospital
Yella Speaks

I hesitated for about three seconds, looking from Steele, to the smashed wine glass on the floor, to Steele again. My immediate thought was, *if I don't start agreeing with him right now, he's going to kill me.* So I went with my instincts and started shamelessly groveling.

"I apologize if I've offended you," I said, bowing my head humbly. "It's the last thing I want to do after the kindness you've shown to me; to us. It's a sensitive subject, I appreciate that. There's been a lot of unnecessary suffering, and that's a terrible thing."

"And that's what pains me. No-one can break that pig spell. No-one. Not even *me*. It's iron-clad and inhumane. Due to unforgiveable evil and wickedness."

"Unimaginable, awful wickedness," I agreed.

"Coming from that woman. And nobody *else,*" he emphasized.

"That's right," I agreed again. "That awful, wicked woman."

"That whore," he spat.

I nodded enthusiastically. "That ruthless, conniving, shameless, leg-spreading bitch."

"Finally, you're starting to see reason." He looked relieved. "I see you're not a complete idiot after all."

"I can see your side of the argument now and the more I think of it, the more sense it's starting to make," I said, nodding again.

"Damn right," he agreed. "And by the way I also *firmly* believe she's dead."

"That's perfectly reasonable and logical too."

"Splendid. She was evil, and now she's dead. Got it?"

"Got it."

He sighed. "I'm pleased that you can be reasoned with, Mister Fella. I must confess, you were beginning to annoy me, but I'm satisfied now that we have reached some sort of agreement. Now then – shut up, come along and follow me before I swat you."

He got up off the lounge and started walking. I followed him like a naughty puppy following its master, swearing I'd just grown fur and big, floppy ears in that moment. I was pathetic. *You've got no balls,* I chided myself. *You just agreed with everything he said and sold your soul for profit like some miserable prostitute.*

What the hell, I answered myself back. *He's a powerful sorcerer, and I've already escaped a country illegally and robbed a man before leaving him to rot for dead, so I may as well be a lying, groveling, immoral man-whore too.*

We walked outside to a large patio area with lounge chairs and a twenty-meter pool and I saw that the entire building was elevated above the ground. There were about thirty steps beyond the pool, leading down to the desert's surface.

The sorcerer stood at the front of the swimming pool and spread his arms in pride. "As I said, I've designed all this myself. Does it please you?"

I nodded with gritted teeth, a whirlpool of emotions churning inside me: worry, fear, frustration, anger. Who gave a toss if it was a palace with a hundred royal virgins? I wanted Petelia back, and

I wanted her back now. She could be dying or worse, and all he could talk about was his stupid building decorations. What was *wrong* with him? Was he a complete idiot? Why was he stalling? Was it wise to keep at him, or should I take off to search for her by myself? And if I did, would he become enraged at my disobedience and kill me for it?

No matter what I did or said, I couldn't get the sorcerer to budge; it was the worst scenario ever. All I could do was hope and pray that Petelia was still alive.

Elsewhere in the Desert

They were close; so close that Petelia could clearly see their open mouths and razor-sharp fangs as they ran towards her. Some had even made it as far as the bottom of the hill. Brown sand giants. A large swarm. Too many to count.

It was only a matter of time.

She was still screaming as her knees gave way beneath her and thudded to the ground. Then it was as if she'd suddenly become a heavy concrete statue – she couldn't move. Oh God, she couldn't move, even though she longed to slash her own throat and die there and then before the dirty savages could get to her. But she had no knife, and her terror had paralyzed her, rendering her useless. And they were only getting closer. Closer!

She knew she was about to die, but couldn't do anything about it. She could only be a witness to her own torture and ultimate demise. They would rape her. Dismember her. They would–

Oh my God! she thought over and over to herself. *Oh my God!*

Warm fluid was gushing down from between her legs. She felt sick. So sick… Suddenly her body felt like it didn't belong to her anymore. It was more like a vibrating, trembling 'thing' she could no longer control. Her heart was pounding hard, as if threatening to break out of her chest at any moment. She tried to breathe, but her throat was closing up – it was constricting her air.

Breathe! she told herself. *Breathe!*

She tried desperately to suck in more air. Then a powerful wave of dizziness came, and she felt the blood drain from her face, seeping and sucking the life away. Her head hit the earth hard after that, but the blackness had already taken her, and she didn't feel a thing.

Desert Hospital
Yella Speaks

The whirlpool of emotions inside me churned, rolled and flipped and finally gave me bigger balls. I was angry, and mentally prepared myself to stand up to the sorcerer and be killed for it if necessary. I had to do *something* to help my friend. After all, wouldn't she do the same for me? Come to think of it, probably not. It didn't matter.

And then a realization came over me; an inner knowing at the core of my bones. For some strange reason, he had no intention of rescuing Petelia, and he was deliberately distracting me by going on and on, talking about rubbish, either trying to impress me with his magic or strike fear in me whenever I mentioned rescuing her. I stared at him, finally deciding that I'd had enough.

He was still talking, as if he had no intention to stop, this time about his stupid nurses.

"Look behind you," he said proudly.

Around ten women, all stunning and in their twenties, filed through the door and formed an orderly line in front of the pool. Each looked almost identical to the other, like a perfect collection of beautiful dolls; all had waist long hair and wore sandals and sarongs with slits at the side. Ample cleavages spilled out of glittery, scanty tops as the women smiled at me with gleaming white teeth.

"What do you think about *that,* eh?" the sorcerer asked, watching my face for a reaction. "Shall we wine with them now?"

"If you don't want to rescue Petelia then fine, I'll search for her myself," I said flatly, looking him squarely in the eye. "I'm tired of waiting and I'm over this rubbish. I'm going now. This minute. Don't try to stop me."

The sorcerer looked surprised at my boldness. "No. You're to stay here with the nurses."

"I'm not staying with anyone! I'm rescuing Petelia, Goddammit!" I shouted, face reddening. "What sort of a man are you? She could be *dying* out there, and you're not doing anything!" I smashed the glass of water I was holding to the floor, not caring anymore if he killed me or not. "I'm getting out of here, and don't try to stop me!" I repeated, pointing at him angrily. "You don't scare me anymore!"

"You'll never make it out of there alive, you damned fool," he said calmly, looking at the pieces of shattered glass on the floor.

"I'm willing to take my chances." I abruptly turned to go.

He clamped a firm hand on my shoulder, stopping me in my tracks. "Searching for your friend is not only a form of suicide, it's a waste of time," he warned. "The sand monsters would have no doubt taken her before I even met you. The area is swarming with them. She wouldn't have stood a chance in hell. I'm sorry."

I paused, letting the terrible words sink in. "And in all the time I've spent with you, in all that time, you couldn't have just been honest and told me that?" I asked, voice straining with emotion.

"Well, they're terrible words that are hard to say."

"Why didn't you speak up?" I struggled against the tears, but my eyes watered anyway. "I don't understand. What the hell's wrong with you?"

"I'm a coward," he admitted with a shrug. "One who avoids such matters."

"A coward and a *bully*," I added.

"Hold your tongue, you cheeky bastard," he snapped. His yellow eyes flashed dangerously. "I never said I was perfect."

I glared at him. "To hell with you *and* your opinions," I spat defiantly. "She's my best friend!" And then I ran like the wind, past him, his team of pretty dollies, and the pool, and was rapidly making my way down the steps when his voice boomed from behind me.

"Sleep!" he commanded. "Sleep!"

And that was the rather short and abrupt end of my solo search mission – I blacked out, and had a nasty bruise on the side of my head when I woke up the next day.

Elsewhere in the Desert

Steele shape-shifted into a bird immediately after directing his nurses to carry Yella to bed, materializing instantly to the spot where he'd seen Rebel's head sticking out of the sand. He guessed Petelia would be close by and soon discovered that indeed, she was not only close by, she was still fully above the ground and possibly even *alive*. He was shocked. What was going on with her? Was she dead, or just unconscious? Not to worry, he'd soon find out. And there was precious little time to get to her, because she was surrounded by scores of sand monsters making their way towards her – he quickly estimated around forty. An extraordinary amount, the most he'd ever seen around a human.

He knew what *they* wanted, the dirty brown bastards.

He had to act fast.

He zeroed down towards her, morphing into human form before even hitting the ground. Efficiently, he had her unconscious form in his arms in only seconds. He knew instantly that she was alive and had most likely only fainted, as his razor-keen senses easily picked up her heartbeat. She stunk of urine.

"Back off!" he barked to the sand monsters. They were only meters away, forming a rough circle around him, and were slowly closing in. "Come any closer and I'll kill you!"

They gasped, not daring to take another step, even though they easily dwarfed him, for as well as knowing who and what he was, his deep, strong voice carried with it a distinct air of power and authority.

"Give her to us. She is ours," a sand monster demanded boldly.

Steele briefly assessed him. One of the biggest, standing at the front, with big everything. Big head. Big shoulders. Big balls. Even bigger mouth. He calmly turned his head and spat out the piece of gum he'd been chewing on. "How *dare* you speak to me like that? Do you forget so easily that I am your lord and master?"

"She is in the territory of the creatures of the sand," the same sand monster pointed out. "She belongs to us."

"And as you are all well aware, I am both the master of this territory *and* the creatures of the sand," Steele shot back. "She belongs to me."

"Your magic cannot hold all of us if we decide to take her," the sand monster threatened.

For the first time in a very long while, Steele felt worried, though he didn't dare show it. He could easily dematerialize with the girl to the hospital, but that would seem to them as running away; an act of cowardice. They would never respect him again, and if there was one thing he could not afford to lose, it was their respect; it was far too dangerous.

But if they did decide to lunge and he decided to save her by killing them all, it would seriously drain a large amount of his magical powers. It would take months to recover from that, and for what? A measly mortal woman he didn't even know.

He could compromise by killing only a few of them, pretend to weaken, then let the rest of them drag the girl into an underground cave. He'd saved many lives in the desert hospital in his time; surely he'd racked up enough karma points to let one life go? What would it matter, to let one life slip? It would only be one measly little life...

One measly little life...

A tiny bead of sweat fell slowly down his forehead as he forced himself to remain calm and logical. He knew if he showed any weakness at all, the hairy brown bastards would try to kill him, so he made sure his tone remained authoritative and strong.

"Listen to me, all of you! You do not need to eat this woman. I will personally supply you with all the meat you desire," he offered.

"We have already feasted. We are not seeking food," the sand monster said as his kind grunted in agreement.

Steele glared at him as he took in the full meaning of the words. "I can hardly believe my ears!" he shouted. "Have your hairy cocks erased your brains? I *forbid* you from pleasuring yourself with this woman, and I could kill all of you in an instant if you defy me, have no doubt about it!"

"You lie," the sand monster said, baring large, sharp fangs with a gravelly snarl. "You lie."

"Then try me, you hairy bastard," Steele challenged, meeting the creature's eyes with a dangerous sneer of his own. "Just try me."

Petelia picked that exact moment to wake up and started whimpering in his arms. It tipped the monsters over from being half-willing to listen to reason to a frenzy of lust, and they collectively howled and charged, powerful muscles tightening, covering large amounts of ground in only seconds. With no time left for the luxury of thinking, Steele held his nerve, stood his ground, and let his powerful magic do its work.

What happened next happened very fast: big mouth was the first to be turned to stone, turning into a giant statue before crackling, crumbling, then rolling downhill. His two closest neighbors were next, and on and on it went, until around thirty or so sand monsters were killed, meeting eternity amidst great sprays of sand and crumbling rock. The rest decided to quickly flee underground; the only ones showing any brains at all.

When it was finally all over, Steele felt gutted, like he'd just survived a great war, the likes of which he'd never experienced. His eyes were stinging and red from the dust that still lingered in the air and he briefly closed them, throwing his head back in sheer exhaustion as the blonde woman clung to him like a limpet and sobbed uncontrollably in his arms.

He literally felt the power draining from his body like a steady stream of flowing water. Not only had his magic taken a nasty hammering that day, his body had too, as they were permanently interlinked. He was so tired he barely knew what to think or feel anymore; and yet the desert around them was now so isolated and peaceful, the only indication of the great battle fought being the dust that still twirled and danced in the air.

When they both finally materialized in the stone hospital, he was far too tired to think of something as petty as decorum and collapsed right on top of Petelia on a double bed in one of the rooms. While he was exhausted, her adrenaline was sky-high, and all her brain could register was that a strange dark-haired man was lying on top of her with sinister intentions to rape. She screamed with all her might, squirming and gasping beneath him.

"Get off me!"

He quickly took ahold of her wrists, pinning her against the mattress. "Calm down for pity's sake! Shush! Calm down! I'm not going to hurt you! Stop!"

She continued wriggling and squirming in his grip as he spoke, screaming defiantly back at him. "Get off me! Get! Off!"

She managed to bite his wrist and he instantly released her from his grip, screaming with pain. He immediately slapped her across the face. "You little bitch! Sleep!" he barked, clicking his fingers.

Dutifully she responded to his magic, closing her eyes and falling instantly into a deep and peaceful sleep, looking nothing like the enraged tigress of only seconds ago.

Meanwhile he carefully inspected his red and throbbing wrist, and was devastated to discover he had to concentrate hard to make the pain go away. Exactly as feared, his powers had been severely weakened.

"You bastard," he murmured darkly.

Chapter Five

The Next Morning
Yella Speaks

I woke at the crack of dawn, my very first thoughts being about the girls. Where were they? Were they alive, and were they safe? It took several tries to find Rebel's room and when I finally did, I raced to her, not even bothering to shut the door behind me. I smiled happily when she stirred in her sleep, and then I couldn't help myself; I called her name and shook her awake. I tried to do it gently, but was way too excited for that, and she grunted in protest, groggily opening her eyes.

"Hey, it's me. Yella. Can you sit up?" I murmured.

"Yeah," she replied weakly, moving slowly, as if it pained her.

"Here. Let me help." I made sure I was gentle this time, easing her slowly into position.

"Where am I?"

"You wouldn't believe how good it is to see you again," I smiled, squeezing her shoulder lightly.

"Wait a second. Did something bad happen?"

I considered her confused brown eyes, smiled, stroked her filthy face and sand-caked hair, and squeezed her shoulder again. "How about I tell you later?"

"How about you tell me *now*? And where's the blonde?"

At that moment a beautiful nurse with long, dark-brown hair, olive skin and brown eyes came into the room without a word, carrying a blue cotton gown and towel in her arms. We both stared as she neatly folded the items, leaving them lying on the bottom of the bed before silently walking out. She came back around five minutes later, carrying a large bowl of soapy water with a sponge floating on top.

"Who's the chick?" Rebel asked. "Is she a servant or something?"

The dark-haired woman carefully put the bowl down on the bedside table, opened her mouth and finally said something. "I'm not a servant," she snapped. "I'm a trained nurse, excellent cook, avid reader, limber dancer, thorough cleaner and very cunning lizard, so kindly mind your manners and don't ever call me a servant again."

"What did you just say?" I asked.

"I just said I wasn't a servant."

"No, after that. Did I hear you just say that you're a *lizard*?"

"Yes. A studdgarta lizard from the Baraktenian Desert. We all are. The master always shape-shifts us when we come to work here." She raised her eyebrows. "Is there some sort of problem with that?"

"Why would he do such a thing?" I asked.

"You'll have to ask *him* that question, won't you? Now get out."

"What?"

"You're getting in the way of my work," she explained irritably. "This woman is my patient and I need to be alone with her to do my duties efficiently. Don't you have something to do?"

At that moment Petelia burst excitedly into the room. "Yella! Rebel!"

The studdgarta stood with her arms crossed, rolling her eyes as the three of us emotionally and noisily hugged and kissed each other. To her credit, she allowed a few precious minutes of bonding before speaking again.

"I find this child-like sentimentality perfectly charming, really I do, but you need to be bathed," she said to Rebel, "and you two need to be fed," she said to Petelia and I. "So go along now and eat your breakfast, it's been prepared for you already." She made a shooing motion with her hands.

"Hey! How come I'm the one that doesn't get fed?" Rebel protested.

"I'll feed you myself – after your sponge bath. You've been badly affected by the storm and you're in a much weaker state than your friends. In view of that, you need to stay exactly where you are." She arched an authoritative eyebrow. "Nurse's orders."

"I don't want to leave Rebel just yet," I protested. "Can't I help in some way?"

"You can help by leaving," she replied. "Your friend's about to have a sponge bath and I suspect she'd like her privacy, don't you? Or shall I tell Master Steele, your most gracious host, that you've insulted him by hindering his hard-working nursing staff?"

She arched an eyebrow again.

"I'll come back later," I replied, admitting defeat.

"Do so," she nodded primly.

Elsewhere in the Desert

The day was just beginning as Steele, in bird form, overlooked the vast desert expanse from the branch of a large dead tree, staring at nothing in particular. Perched on a branch just above him was Paraklii, a chubby, bright purple bird with a large, pointy beak. They'd been friends for many years, even though he was odd-looking, with very little intellect and no magical powers whatsoever. He was singing, as he usually did first thing in the morning, as Steele attended to very pressing, important matters: feeling desperately sorry for himself.

He knew full well that killing around thirty giant furry creatures would drain his powers, but the sand monster with the big mouth had, thank God, severely underestimated his magical strength. Miraculously it still held strong, though it had been severely weakened, and would take months to recover.

He'd felt half-dead from exhaustion the night before and wanted nothing more than sleep, but the blonde woman had gone all feral and bit him, inadvertently kicking off a rage that had sent a second shot of adrenaline through his veins.

Another thing that had set him off last night was seeing the evidence of his severely weakened powers with his very own eyes. Almost mad with rage, he immediately materialized to his house in the Sarakonian mountains, where he preceded to storm through the rooms, rant and rave and throw things, wake his girlfriend up, kick her precious cat so hard it flew, and then smash almost everything they owned to pieces. Then he had a nasty fight with her, a very nasty fight, where she screamed, kicked him in the balls and left him. He'd deal with her later. The cat, meanwhile, took quick refuge in the garden – how he hated that animal.

Alone in the house, minus girlfriend and cat, and doubled over with pain from the cruel blow to his nether regions, he eventually managed to heal his body with magic and calm himself.

Why not spend the rest of the night doing something useful, he thought, *like calculating the power lost in the fight with the sand monsters?* It sounded like a sensible idea to him, so he spent the rest of the night carefully testing and re-testing his magic. After several hours of testing and with a quickly sinking heart, he finally had an estimation of the damage done to his magic by the time the sun rose: he'd lost around one fourth of his powers.

One fourth.

One *Goddamn* fourth.

The amount was huge, and even though he knew he'd eventually heal and recover from the power drain, the healing process would still take several months. And that was devastating, like trying to come to terms with suddenly losing two perfectly good legs, or even worse, a cock. It didn't feel real, but he only had to do his magic and feel its severely weakened force to be reminded of his terrible fight with the sand monsters.

The past was the past though, and he couldn't do a thing about it – except, of course, yell and throw things, smash his entire house up, have a fight with his girlfriend, and kick her stupid cat – which he'd already done.

He could have killed the girl instantly and it still would have taught the lusty sand monsters a lesson, as they would be denied their prize. Or he could have swallowed his pride, let the sand monsters be and dematerialized to the hospital with the girl. Or he could have just assessed the situation when he saw it from the skies and let the sand monsters have their way with her – that would have been the best option ever.

She was a little mortal bitch anyway. He had risked everything, selflessly saving her miserable little life, only for her to suddenly turn into a vicious attack dog and bite him. And he was lavishly housing and entertaining her at this very moment, with his studdgarta pets playing nurses and servants. The very thought of it made him feel ill.

He knew Yella was a wanted man, and that the other two were civilian outlaws. He knew he could easily get his revenge by delivering the mortal trio to the soldiers. The psychic Jet Black had promised the sexual services of the beautiful soldier Klo as a reward for doing so, and what man wouldn't want *her*? Didn't the soldiers owe him their very lives? Didn't he deserve to be rewarded for his good efforts for a change?

A small, quiet voice in his mind chastised him for being so mean and childish while another voice badly ached for the sweet taste of revenge. And yet another voice wanted both of them to shut up. It hurt to think so much sometimes... It hurt...

Everything Goddamn hurt.

He immediately sensed that Paraklii was about to fly off. "Don't go," he said quickly.

"I sense your bad mood," Paraklii said. "The air reeks of it. It's foul."

"Don't go," Steele repeated stubbornly.

"Give me a good reason to stay."

"Very well. I'm finished with thinking; it hurts my head too much. And I could do with a song or two."

"Not good enough. Give me another reason," his friend insisted.

"Very well," Steele repeated, gritting his teeth. "How about I've just been bitten on the wrist, kicked in the balls, lost one fourth of my total magical powers and been dumped by my girlfriend, and the only thing in the world that could possibly cheer me up right now is the relaxing sound of your voice. Will that do?"

"Alright then."

"Then what are you waiting for? *Sing,* you stupid purple-feathered bastard!" Steele barked. "Before I lose my patience and feed you to a sand monster. Sing!"

So Paraklii sang like he'd never sung before, preferring not to be ripped apart and eaten alive that sunny morning.

❧

Desert Hospital
Yella Speaks

Petelia and I walked to the main area to find wonderful, proper food laid out on the wooden table: nuts and fruits of all kinds, buttered bread, honeyed porridge, fried eggs and tomatoes, and orange juice and tea. Well, let's just say that not only did we look like two dirty feral pigs, we ate like them too. Later, after what felt like an eternity of being dirty and gross, we were ordered to wash ourselves in separate rooms. When it was all over, it was undeniably wonderful to be clean again, as if my skin could finally breathe after a weight had been lifted from it.

Most of the time the studdgartas seemed to be in the kitchen area, either preparing meals or cleaning for us, and I marveled at the sorcerer's abundant generosity. He'd obviously forced me to stay in the hospital out of kindness and he'd finally gotten around to rescuing Petelia. I was beyond grateful to him for saving us and was looking forward to seeing him again, despite our former differences. Maybe we could start over and become real friends this time? And maybe I could convince him to transport us all to Sarakonia?

When I made my way over to Rebel's room to check on her, the same studdgarta was carefully hand-feeding her grapes. She'd been thoroughly washed and was now wearing a light blue cotton gown, and her formerly dirt-caked black hair shone glossily.

"Oh," the studdgarta said when she saw me, looking disappointed. "It's *you* again."

"Do you mind leaving so I can talk to Rebel alone?" I asked, getting straight to the point.

"A good nurse never leaves her patient," she answered.

So that was a definite no. "I suppose I can't insult our most gracious host by going against the wishes of his nurse?"

"Indeed," she responded. "And he also doesn't like injured and weakened patients being bothered by overly enthusiastic visitors. Did he not mention this fact to you?"

"Can't I at least talk with her for a little while? She's a good friend of mine. I'd really appreciate it."

"I suppose so," she said reluctantly.

"Thanks," I said. "You're a very hard working, dedicated nurse."

"And you sir," she said sourly as she got up from her chair, "are a smart ass."

I was hoping by some miracle she'd change her mind and leave the room so I could be alone with Rebel, but no such luck. She walked towards the door and stood in the corner with her arms folded like a loyal watchdog.

Rebel was sitting upright in her hospital bed, her back supported by two big pillows. "Don't mind the nurse chick," she said cheerfully. "She's just being protective, that's all. It's good to see ya."

"And even better to see you," I replied, leaning in and kissing her on the cheek. "You're looking much stronger now." I sat on the chair by the bed. "The strength's even there in your voice."

"Whatever. Just don't ask me to fight off another storm right now."

I smiled. "You've been told of the sorcerer who rescued us? Quite an interesting character, that one."

"Oh yeah," Rebel nodded. "We had a great chit-chat this

morning, didn't we, sweetheart?" She turned to the studdgarta, who grunted curtly in response.

"Reaching Sarakonia's now a sure thing with a sorcerer helping us," I said.

"Nothing's a sure thing, Yella Fella. Learnt that when I was in the army."

"Not even with sorcerers?"

"*Especially* not even with sorcerers. They're a temperamental bunch of bastards."

The studdgarta arched a questioning eyebrow from her corner and Rebel noticed it.

"Except for Steele Silver of course," she added quickly. "What a great and gracious man he is. By the way, I don't like this stupid idea you have of tracking the Queen down in Sarakonia. Don't you realize how dangerous that is?"

"Why are we suddenly on this subject?"

"You saved my life, sweetheart," she answered. "I'd kinda like to save yours too. Do you like being tortured till you're begging to die?"

"Not at all."

"'Cause that's what'll happen if the soldiers discover us. You're famous, I'm infamous. They already know what we look like and you and me, we done the worst crime you can ever commit in Barakten. We betrayed its ruler and that's very serious. If they found us, they'd probably *invent* a new torture method, just to make us suffer more. You got that?"

"Don't you think I've heard all the torture stories too?"

"And you still want to risk your life to find her?"

"Yes."

"What are you? Insane?" She paused thoughtfully. "Oh I get it, I get it."

"What?"

"You think finding her will get you off the hook for escaping Barakten, right? You think it'll spare you from punishment – that they'll leave you alone and then you'll go home unmolested. Maybe even get some sort of medal?"

"No, that's not–"

"Well there won't be no medals, I'm telling ya. They'll kill you 'cause that's what they're trained to do. A betrayal's a betrayal, rules are rules. Holy fuck. Do you think these guys have things like morals and reasoning powers? Are you assuming they actually have brains?"

"Then I'll find a way of leading the Queen to the soldiers without being discovered, won't I?"

"You wanna settle down in Sarakonia, don'tcha?"

"You know I do."

"Then why don't you just concentrate on something sensible and noble when you get there, like putting your head down and working hard? Forgetting about her and settling down? Beats me why you care about her so much anyway," she mumbled. "She's a mean bitch–"

"That's what everyone thinks, and it's not the truth," I interrupted, crossing my arms over my chest.

"Aww come on," Rebel argued. "She's so evil I can almost see the horns growing out of her head."

"None of your theories are true."

"Then enlighten me. Tell me why you wanna waste time tracking her down. I'm all ears."

I took a big breath as I launched into the explanation. "It's partly professional. I was given an assignment to find her and I want to finish that assignment."

"You're obviously not working for the court officials anymore," she pointed out.

"That's right I'm not. But I'm still working for me."

"So it's a professional pride thing, right?"

"Something like that."

"Okay. So what's the other reason?"

"I feel," I hesitated, "bonded to her. We've shared many past lifetimes together."

"Yeah?" She arched a cynical eyebrow. "*That* sounds like a lotta fun."

"But I don't know any other details and to be honest, I'm tired of trying to understand something that may never be fully understood. I've decided to hell with it, give in – give in to my feelings instead of fighting them."

"Your feelings?"

I nodded. "They're like an itch, planted in my heart, begging to be scratched."

She raised her eyebrows. "An *itch*?"

"Yes."

"An *itch*," she repeated, as if she didn't hear me properly the first time.

"Yes."

She closed her eyes and held a hand up, appearing to concentrate. "Okay, let me get this straight: you're willing to risk your life, throw everything to the dogs, and get brutally tortured for an *itch*?"

"It's a mystery to me too but–"

"The only *mystery* is why I happen to like you so much. You're totally fucking crazy!"

"Hold it right there!" the studdgarta bellowed from the corner.

We turned our heads to stare at the annoying presence I'd temporarily forgotten.

"That will be enough energetic chit-chat for now, thank you very much," she said primly. "You're exciting my patient with your arguing, and that's not very good for her in her weakened state."

"Not turning out to be much fun, are you?" I sighed.

"I'm a *nurse*," she reminded me. "I'm not supposed to be any fun. Now run along and play in the other room with your silly blonde friend, will you? I need to attend to my patient."

"One helluva bodyguard, isn't she?" Rebel said, laughing.

"Nurse," the studdgarta corrected.

"Alright," I conceded. "No more arguing, some things are nearly impossible to explain anyway. Even to myself. I'll drop by later to see how you are," I said, rolling my eyes at the exceedingly annoying lizard and giving Rebel's hand a quick, affectionate squeeze.

The studdgarta was not impressed. "You're a pain."

"And you're starting to be an even bigger one," I said before I left.

The sorcerer had done everything for us and was spoiling us with food and drink and nurses, but I was already looking forward to getting the hell out of the hospital and getting on with my life. Being ordered around by a know-it-all leathery animal masquerading as a beautiful human was getting tiresome to say the least.

Hours later, after more afternoon chit-chat and eating with Petelia and the other studdgarta nurses in the lounge room, I needed to pee (too much orange juice) so I was walking towards the back entrance to relieve myself when I came yet again upon the same studdgarta. And yet again, she kept to her predictable habit of being annoying by blocking my path.

"Please, I need to relieve myself," I protested irritably. "Can you let me pass?"

"I'd like to apologize," she said, the unexpected words rapidly tumbling from her mouth. "I think I've been far too hard on you. You were just trying to be a good friend to Rebel and I was being most difficult. I'm not normally like this, you know. I have a fun side."

"It's quite alright," I said, remembering the sorcerer's hospitality and my own manners. "You were just trying to do your job and I appreciate it. No harm done. I apologize also for my sarcasm."

"Indeed," she nodded. "I was just trying to be a good lizard. You do understand that, don't you?" Her large, liquid brown eyes looked at me pleadingly. "I'm very passionate about what I do and passion is a good thing, but it can also get in the way sometimes. Because it's also my duty to make you feel comfortable here and I happen to be failing at that miserably. I've been far too focused on Rebel."

"You *are* a good lizard," I assured her, "and a fine nurse too. And can I also say that you've got very nice eyes." *And can I also say that I really need to pee right now and you're getting in my way?* I thought irritably.

"My name's Tatiana." She smiled and nodded.

"Pleased to meet you," I replied, nodding back politely. "Now I really must–"

"Wait!" She quickly held her hands up. "I'm off duty now that I've given Rebel her dinner and I'd very much like to cook for you, would you like that? No, don't answer that, I've already decided for you so what would you like to eat?"

"That's very kind of you," I said. "I'll have anything without meat. Now can I–"

She looked truly shocked. "You sound like a vegetarian. Are you a vegetarian?"

"Yes. Now can I please–"

"Vegetarian humans are such a rarity, are they not?" she asked, an even brighter smile lighting up her face. "We studdgartas love vegetarian humans as they pose no threat to us. We've been eaten by humans before. Our meat is very tasty, you know."

"I'll take your word for it as I'll never know. The very thought of eating meat makes me sick. Now can I–"

These words seemed to please her even more, so she grabbed my hand and immediately started kissing it, warm, moist pecking lips making their way past the hand and up the arm. "You wonderful (peck, peck) vegetarian (peck, peck) man," she said. "It's such an honor (peck, peck) to serve you."

"Tatiana," I said wearily. "Please let go of my arm, stop kissing me and let me urinate."

"As you wish," she said, smiling brightly again. She gave me one last, final peck – a quick kiss on the cheek, and then left, making her way back to the kitchen.

After I finally relieved myself, I felt tired, so I napped in my room for about an hour and when I came out, I saw Petelia in the corridor. A different Petelia to usual; my jaw practically dropped to the floor when I saw her. She'd obviously been busy getting ready for dinner and had done a spectacular job, all make-up, clean hair and pink dress. Her freshly washed hair was shiny, thick and lustrous, and I suppressed a sudden urge to play with it, to run my fingers through the long, golden strands.

"You look beautiful," I said, looking her up and down.

She ignored my compliment and linked an arm through mine. "So many things have happened since we've been separated and we desperately need to talk," she said seriously, steering me towards the lounge room. "I mean really talk – *alone*. Without any nurses hovering around and butting in all the time. Let's find a corner by ourselves somewhere."

"Let's do it," I agreed, patting her arm. "I've got a lot of things to tell you."

"Trust me, I've got even more."

"Alright then. You go," I offered. "Ladies first."

So we made our way down the corridor together, talking animatedly, starting an intense conversation that went on for hours.

~~~

Several Hours Later

Tatiana, busily cooking in the kitchen, smiled wickedly to herself as she slowly stirred and smelt the simmering contents of a delicious homemade soup, consisting of stock, water, onions, herbs, vegetables, and magical love potion.

She'd wanted Yella from the moment she laid eyes on him; she'd merely been playing hard to get. Well the time for games was well and truly over. Thanks to the love potion he was as good as hers, and she was going to have him very, very soon. Within hours. The love potion was incredibly strong, and would make him either act out his lust, or go mad denying it. She guessed he'd choose the former, as men tended to do. She was so excited she could barely suppress a giggle.

Like Master Steele, Yella had a wonderful scent; it was sweet and spicy and felt like warm honey flowing down her sex, making it throb with a wonderful aliveness and longing. She wondered what sort of lover he'd be. Gentle or fierce? Loud or subtle? Fast or slow? Would he match Master Steele? No man had ever matched Master Steele, though they'd been so much fun, as all inhibitions and insecurities disappeared when the love potion coursed through their bodies.

Being a human at the hospital wasn't easy. She had to pretend to be something she wasn't, to please Master Steele. Master Steele wanted professionalism, so she was prim and proper. He wanted all tasks done perfectly, so she was disciplined and bossy. He wanted seriousness, so she hardly ever smiled. He wanted detachment, so she appeared cold. She loved Master Steele (and loved his manhood even more) but he could be a very particular boss. No matter. Tonight, she would be a different sort of human, the sort of human she much preferred: a warm, fun, talkative, sexy human. Now *that* was far more interesting. And Yella could finally get to see her as she really was; no more silly acting.

Despite his flaws, Master Steele was very sympathetic to her human desires when she worked at the hospital, so gifted her with the magic love potion several years ago to use on the men of her choice. So long as they weren't sick and were well enough to have sex, it was all fine with him. He liked to see his studdgarta pets enjoy themselves. He even liked to watch occasionally.

As far as she was concerned, humans had a lot to glean from the wisdom of lizards. Lizards didn't care about petty things like clothes or kitchen utensils or table manners. They didn't make an immediate fuss of getting a bit of dirt on themselves. They didn't care about how their bodies looked or about passing wind in public or about having sex in front of each other. They didn't feel the stupid and useless human emotion of shame. Humans were far too fussy and prudish and inhibited for their own good. And anyway, the only one that could possibly be offended by the effects of the love potion would be his silly little blonde friend, and who cared about *her*?

❧

Evening
Yella Speaks

Petelia and I were eating dinner and drinking wine at the kitchen table with six other studdgartas (the rest were waiting on us), and she was ignoring every single one of them as she talked almost non-stop about her desert ordeal.

"I'm so sorry you had to go through that," I said, taking her hand in mine and pressing my lips against her knuckles. "I tried to get Steele to help you earlier, I really did, but like a big coward, I let him get to me. I'm so sorry. Can you ever forgive me?"

"Don't be silly," she replied. "There's nothing to forgive, and nothing you could have done."

"You're my best friend," I reminded her. "I should've tried to search for you a lot earlier than what I did."

We looked at each other then, my lips still firmly pressed against her knuckles. The gaze was a little too long, and for the first time I saw Petelia, not as a sister who'd become dear to me, but as a woman who stirred feelings of lust. Suddenly embarrassed and self-conscious, I let her hand go and quickly changed the subject. My thoughts seemed to be taking on a strange life of their own – I was surprised to find my hands curling themselves into tight fists, straining against reaching out and touching her, fighting off sudden waves of desire. A very weird and uncomfortable feeling. I cleared my throat and hid my hands under the table, but my desire must've burned in my eyes as we talked, because she suddenly blushed, turned away, said she needed to pee, and took off.

In a short amount of time, a ridiculously short amount of time, I'd grown very fond of Petelia – a woman from a very different world to mine. There was no-one on the planet I wanted to be with or talk to more than Petelia; for better or worse, she'd become my closest confidant and dearest friend. What was happening, I wondered. Was I falling in love with her too?

As I tried to make sense of my thoughts, Tatiana wasted no time in taking Petelia's place; she sat alongside me with a beaming smile, and soon the evening was awash with sounds of girlish laughter, animated conversation and lively music. I looked over and saw Petelia smiling and rapt in conversation, seemingly content in the company of the studdgartas. I was more than content; I was smiling from ear to ear like a boy with a sweet tooth and a bag of chocolate. I noticed my wine cup being constantly topped up, but by that time I was having far too much of a good time talking to the most beautiful women I'd ever seen in my life to care.

As the evening wore on, I unfortunately got very drunk, so drunk I could only remember fragments of my conversation with Tatiana. She looked absolutely stunning in a glittery crop top and sarong and her long, dark hair was unfettered and shone in the candlelight. For some reason she was a different person that night, a person I didn't recognize but really liked. A warm, funny, intelligent person that was nice to be around.

She was a great listener too, which was also nice, so I found myself offloading and telling her everything; how hard it was growing up being different, how I had very few friends in childhood and how even my own parents had discouraged my gift. How I escaped Barakten and met a psychic spice merchant in the desert. How he tried to kill me and was now stalking me telepathically. How the Queen was never far from my thoughts and how I'd always been fascinated by her. How I felt a strong connection to her.

And suddenly I felt my lust switch from Petelia to Tatiana, just like that. Sweet Lord, I was like a dog with a new leg to hump! I remember feeling so sexually attracted to Tatiana it actually hurt, like a throbbing ache that cried for relief, and wondered what the hell was going on with me. As if to torture me even further, she started teasing me, putting her hand on my knee and stroking my leg – slowly stroking my leg. It was a sweet sort of torture. I felt myself starting to melt under her touch, like snow under a scorching sun.

"Do you know the psychic spice merchant even suggested at one point that the Queen was my destiny?" I told her, struggling to stay focused on what I was saying.

"Oh yes," she replied. She was still stroking my leg, and I was still enjoying it. "I think I do remember you saying something like that earlier."

"And if that happens to be true," I said, slurring my words as I leaned forward and stared at her generous chest, "I mean, if the Queen really is my destiny, then I, Tittyana, am in big trouble."

"*Tat*iana," she corrected, gently pushing me back and lifting my chin up so that I looked at her eyes.

"Sorry. *Tat*iana. Because you know what she'll do?"

"No, what?"

"She'll keep on tormenting me till I've fulfilled my destiny. In other words, drive me mad. Like I've said before, she's an itch in my heart that won't go away. What if I never find her? Whaddoo I do then?"

She smiled, eyes glinting mischievously. "Maybe there's another woman in your destiny too," she murmured, leaning towards me and putting my face in her hands.

We were so close our noses were almost touching. I could almost *taste* her.

"Maybe she can scratch that itch…" She looked at me intimately with her beautiful brown eyes. "Maybe she can even make it…go away…"

Five Seconds Later

Something inside me cracked and burst open like a dam and sweet Lord I lost it. Every single quality that ever made me human. All my inhibitions, all my senses of decency and modesty and respect and control and possibly my entire brain as well. The whole table was probably pointing and laughing at me too, but at that point I didn't notice and didn't really give a shit. I hadn't a hope in hell of controlling the wild beast that had suddenly come into me and oh, that beast, it was enjoying itself.

I kissed Tatiana so hard it felt like I was eating her instead of kissing her; I had her hair in my fist to get a good, tight grip. It was a long and amorous kiss and by the time we finally released each other, our breathing was heavy and ragged.

We straddled the long wooden seat by the table as we faced each other, the lust melting away all sense of pretension between us. She smiled and drew me to her and I felt her softness and warmth again. Then my fingers became ravenous and seemed to pulse, as if lit up and burning, warming the entire room with their presence, fully alive and blazing and starving for more skin; wanting to sink into breasts and hair and lips.

The rest of the world disappeared as I moaned loudly, like the animal I was, and dear God, I lifted her top, pulling it way past the nipples, and had my way with her, eagerly fondling her naked breasts.

If only she would have slapped me across the face, called me names or bit or scratched me. Or even said 'no' and just pushed me away. But no such luck. On the contrary, she returned my lust just as boldly; her bejeweled, manicured hand went straight down the trousers! My teeth clenched as the desire hit me with even greater force, filling me to the core.

I was hard and throbbing and my heart pounded heavily in my chest; I wanted her I wanted her I wanted her sweet Lord I wanted her. And nothing would stop me having her; not the words lying somewhere in my head that were protesting weakly, not the opinions of the others around me and no, not even my own decency, it didn't stand a chance. The animal in me was too strong.

She grabbed the back of my head and greedily clamped me to her smooth brown chest; obligingly I put my mouth on her and ardently kissed, licked and suckled, and she moaned loudly in the pleasure of it.

Then I ripped her top completely off, carelessly tossing it to the side, and started quickly taking my clothes off too, with the full intention of doing her there and then in front of everyone and enjoying every single second of it, so by the time Petelia made her way over to where I was sitting, I was half-naked, panting like a dog, and felt like my cock was on fire.

Then Petelia single-handedly ruined everything: she tapped me hard on the shoulder and when I turned around, I got a full jug of cold water thrown straight in my face!

"What was *that* for?" I spluttered.

"Come on, get up, get up," she snapped, gripping my arm and quickly dragging me away from the table. I vaguely remember a room full of excited studdgartas eagerly clapping and cheering as we walked off. "What the hell do you think you're doing?" she hissed when we were out of ear shot.

She was still firmly gripping my arm. I think I said, "Nothing much, just falling in love with a lizard with very nice eyes and I'm going back to the table now, 'cause I want to kiss her again, 'cause it's been six months since I've been with a woman and I...I..."

She held me firmly by the shoulders and shook me before I could even finish what I was saying. "She's a lizard?" she asked, a serious look coming over her face. "What are you talking about?" She shook me again. "Yella?"

"I kept on meaning to tell you," I slurred. "They're studdgarta lizards from the Baraktenian Desert. All of them. The sorcerer shape-shifted them for us as part of his *hospitality*."

The look on her face was priceless. I couldn't help myself, I started laughing, then burped loudly.

"That sick, sorcerer bastard," she said in disgust.

"That sick, sorcerer bastard," I echoed. "You are *so* right. Now if you'll excuse me, I'll think I'll just get back to what I was doing."

"She's a *lizard*!" Petelia exclaimed, looking horrified.

I shook my head as I swayed a little. "Forget everything I just said," I slurred. "No mention of that word. Tonight, she's nothing but a full-blooded woman, and what a woman she is! No harm done while she's human, right?"

Petelia slapped me hard across the face and then shook me even harder; she was pretty strong for a girl. "Wrong! Listen to me, you stupid drunken idiot. You are *not* going anywhere *near* that damn filthy desert animal. Do you hear me?" she barked. "Do you hear me?"

That was the last thing I remembered before waking up in bed the next day.

The Following Morning
Rebel Speaks

I opened my eyes at the crack of dawn like I always did, but this time I was amazed to feel back to full strength again. I wasn't stupid. I knew magic had saved my life; courtesy of the power of the dark-haired sorcerer guy what's-his-name-still-can't-remember that I hadn't met yet and still wanted to meet. I'd been one very, very lucky bitch.

I got up, dressed, then made my way down the corridor and found myself in a big room with a kitchen in it. I saw a few nurse chicks busily preparing food. One of them came up to me; she was cute. She had long, curly brown hair and blue eyes.

"Good morning, Miss Red." She smiled cheerfully. "I trust you slept well last night?"

"Yeah," I answered, looking her up and down. "Like a rock. Thanks."

"Please, sit down on the lounge and make yourself comfortable. We're just preparing breakfast now. Would you care for some porridge and tea?"

"You bet. Where are the others?"

"I'm not sure to be honest. Still sleeping, I suspect. We'll check on them soon, as they must rise to meet our master. He'll be coming to meet you all this morning."

"I take it you're referring to the sorcerer guy?"

"Indeed," she said, smiling. "He's very much looking forward to meeting you."

"Likewise," I nodded. "And about time too, I might add."

I heard some loud noises coming from the corridor later when I was eating, and all the nurse chicks ran to investigate. Someone was getting excited about something. I was pretty sure I heard both male and female voices, so I assumed the sorcerer was already there, talking to some nurses. Or Petelia. Or Yella. Whatever. I didn't care; I kept right on eating. I was starving for that porridge – I didn't give a rat's ass if an *earthquake* was going on over there.

Yella Speaks

Groaning with a sore head, I slowly opened my eyes to find Petelia in bed alongside me; bright eyed, fully awake and dressed in a frilly white nightgown. She was sitting with her back against the bed-head, her legs hidden beneath the sheets.

"Good morning," she said cheerfully.

I noted I was bare-chested so I lifted the sheet, quickly checking I had my trousers on before asking, "What happened to me last night?"

"You were really drunk and making a fool of yourself, so I threw cold water on you and dragged you off to my room to sleep," she answered matter-of-factly. "You were out like a light after that."

Visions of my out-of-control clinch with Tatiana last night suddenly flooded into my mind and my face flushed hotly. I closed my eyes. "Tell me something, please."

"Yes?" she asked in a cheerful, sing-song voice.

"Tell me last night didn't happen...that I didn't fondle a magnificent pair of breasts...that I didn't start taking my clothes off in front of everyone so we could–"

She laughed. "Do you also want me to say that she didn't put her hands down your trousers and wrap her fingers around your cock?"

So many words rushed to my head in that moment.

"Oh shit," were the only words that came out of my mouth.

"Exactly," she agreed.

I felt like I was going to die from shame, but there was nowhere to run, nowhere to hide, and no hole to sink into. *Holy crap,* I thought.

"I don't understand," I said, turning on my side to face her. "I've never acted that way with a woman. That wasn't me last night. It wasn't *me,* dammit."

She arched a cynical eyebrow. "Well, it sure *looked* like you."

I rolled onto my back, staring at the ceiling in horror. "Sweet Lord, kill me," I said. "For I am an animal and need to be destroyed."

"I couldn't agree more."

"This is disgusting. I've got to apologize to Tatiana," I said quickly, and tried to get up, but Petelia stopped me with a firm hand on my chest, pushing me down.

"Don't bother, it's not going to do you any good."

"What are you talking about?"

Suddenly Petelia's eyes became as blank and as vacuous as a doll's as she shook my arm continuously. "We're in a dream, silly. We're in a dream, silly. We're in a dream, silly. We're in a dream, silly. We're in a–"

Chapter Six

Petelia kept shaking me, telling me to wake up, and I finally sat up groggily before quickly looking under the sheets, checking I still had my trousers on. They were on alright, and Petelia was still wearing the same white, frilly nightgown I saw in my dream. I shook my head a bit as I ran my fingers through my hair, quickly trying to adjust myself to the real world.

Steele and his team of doll-like studdgartas were standing in the corner in front of the opened bedroom door, and judging by the look on his face, he wasn't pleased. He paused for a few seconds, glaring at us while we sat in bed together, as silent and motionless as two stunned deer.

"I save you from certain death, provide you with nursing staff to cater to your every need, and this," he pointed at us in disgust, "*this* is how you repay me?"

"And I cooked you a perfectly decent vegetable soup," Tatiana added coldly.

I briefly met her eyes and immediately felt flooded with a deep, crushing shame.

"Why did you do this?" Steele asked, as if I'd just seduced his girlfriend or wife. "Did I not give you plenty of other women to play with?"

"All you *gave* me was what I didn't want," I told him, still groggy from lack of sleep and nursing a headache. "You gave me an *illusion*."

I regretted saying the words as soon as they left my mouth. Tatiana immediately looked as if I'd just struck her sharply across the face, then ran out of the room.

"Tatiana I'm sorry! Come back!" I shouted, punching the mattress in frustration at my colossally big mouth and even bigger stupidity. "Dammit!"

"Nice work, psychic. As well as offending me, you've also managed to offend one of my pets," Steele snarled. "Whose only crime happened to be slaving her ass off for you and showing you a good time," he added.

Then things went from bad to worse: Petelia decided to speak. "What is your problem?" she demanded. "Why are you so offended? Yella and I only slept in the same bed together. We didn't make love, but even if we did, what in heaven's name is the crime in that?"

The sorcerer stared at her thoughtfully for a few seconds. "Leave us!" he barked to the remaining studdgartas. They retreated hastily.

"Do you not remember the conversation I had with the forty or so sand monsters intent on raping you and tearing you apart?" he asked calmly once we were alone. "Do you not remember me saying" – I blinked and he suddenly materialized sitting cross-legged at the foot of our bed – "that I am the master of this territory, which means you belong to me?"

"What does *that* mean?" she asked, looking confused.

"It *means*," he explained patiently, "that your blue-eyed psychic friend here should not even be sharing the same bed as you. Not without consulting me first, as that sort of privilege is for me, and me only. Do you understand? You are my property for as long as you remain in this territory, which means that I am now your master. I effectively *own* you, and you must do as I say, or suffer the consequences."

"I don't know what you're talking about. Leave me alone," Petelia whispered, her voice trembling.

The sorcerer materialized instantly again, but this time he was even closer to Petelia; he was now sitting on her lap and straddling her. We both automatically jerked back, startled. He leaned in close, his face only inches from hers. "I've just lost one fourth of my powers saving your pretty little ass," he murmured, looking her up and down and running his fingers through her long, golden hair. "And as your master, I think I deserve some sort of payment for it, don't you?"

"I don't get it," she said, wide-eyed as a child and stammering. "How do you want me to pay you?"

He slowly ran a hand down her face. "Not too bright, are you?"

"Get your hands off her and leave her alone," I said evenly. It was brave of me to say it, but I still gulped.

"Or what?" he scoffed.

"I don't find you attractive," Petelia suddenly blurted.

His hands immediately left her. "You don't find me attractive," he repeated, a hard look suddenly coming into his eyes. "Well that's just wonderful. Can you possibly offend and insult me any further?"

Our lives were obviously at stake, so I desperately tried to say something, *anything* to defuse his anger. "You're pleasant enough looking though," I said. "I'm sure someone *else* will find you–"

"Shuttup!" he barked.

"I'm not your whore," Petelia snapped.

"No, it seems someone else's," he shot back.

"How dare you!"

"You know what?" he said, getting off the bed and walking to the door, "I'm tired of both of you. I have neither the time nor the patience for your dull-witted company."

We looked at each other for a few seconds before looking back at him.

"What are you planning on doing?" I asked.

"You'll find out soon enough," he said ominously, slamming the door behind him.

My stomach immediately dropped with an awful, heavy feeling of dread, but I instinctively felt I had little time, so I moved like the wind, springing out of bed and scrounging around the room for my shoes and the rest of my clothes. We were going somewhere; I knew it in the core of my bones. I didn't know exactly where we were going, but wherever it was, we wouldn't be in the hospital for much longer.

"What's he gonna do?" Petelia asked, hugging herself tightly, looking more and more like a trapped animal with each passing second.

"Get out of bed," I said urgently, still scanning the room for the rest of my clothes. "Quickly! Get dressed and gather your things. We're about to move."

Five Minutes Later

Rebel, Petelia and I suddenly went from standing in a luxurious, fully-furnished stone hospital to standing in a vast, arid desert, with only flat, rocky ground beneath us and blue, cloudless skies above. I looked around with a sickening feeling creeping and crawling its way through my stomach as silence surrounded us with a mighty, invisible cloak.

It felt so evil, the silence. Even more than the hostile wilderness waiting to take us, to claim our bones. Even more than the sand that housed vicious, man-eating monsters. It contained something destructive for all of us, I knew it. I felt it.

Something was going to come from the silence. Oh God. And this time there'd be no escape, no–

"What the fuck just happened?" Rebel demanded, pacing restlessly.

"I think the sorcerer teleported us here," I said, stating the obvious. "He sort of propositioned Petelia. She rejected him. He got offended…"

"I didn't find him attractive," Petelia added sheepishly.

"Great! Just great!" she shouted, looking at the two of us. "What the *hell* are we gonna do now?"

"Rebel," I scolded. "Calm down!"

"Whaddaya mean, *calm down*?" she shouted again. "I was starving and didn't even get to finish my own fucking porridge!"

"We'll find a way–"

"How?" she interrupted. "We got no food, no water, no transport and no supplies!"

"There must be *something* we can do," I argued.

"Sure, mister psychic!" she yelled. "Can you meditate now and pull a market stall out of your ass?" She pushed hard against my chest, causing me to take a few steps back.

Then she turned to Petelia, and her mad eyes seemed to burn a hole through her body. "And you! You! *You!*"

"It's not my fault!" Petelia screamed.

"Not your fault? Do you realize how *screwed* we are now?"

"I didn't find him attractive," Petelia blurted for the second time.

Rebel lunged at her furiously, going straight for the neck, and viciously started choking her. "He was a *sorcerer*, you idiot! You could've at least *tried* to find him fucking attractive!"

Petelia was as helpless as a baby under the strength of that iron grip, and I'm not sure she would've stopped if I hadn't intervened. I came up from behind, grabbed Rebel by the wrists and wrenched her hands off by force. "Get off her!" I barked.

"Eat this!" she barked back, twisting her wrists out of my grip with lightning speed and following up with a perfectly sharp elbow to my guts. I howled in pain.

"She's the reason we're in this mess," she said, pointing at Petelia with a shaky finger.

"Horseshit," I panted. "What hope has any of us got against the darkness of magic?"

"She made the sorcerer angry! She should've gone with him! He could've saved–"

"She doesn't have to prostitute herself to please him, you, or anyone!" I interrupted. "Piss off and leave her alone!"

She then pointed a finger at me, trembling with a rage I'd not seen in her before. "You're nothing but a fool with a broken dream," she snarled.

"You don't know what you're talking about," I shot back.

And so the shouting match continued, with Rebel and I circling each other like animals, she wild-eyed and waving her hands about, and I red-faced and screaming myself almost hoarse.

"You'll get yourself killed for your stupid 'quest' to save the Queen!" she shouted. "You're playing with fire and you won't win this time!"

"What the hell have my personal concerns got to do with you?"

She spread her arms dramatically and shrugged. "I'm sorry, I'm an idiot! I happen to care for you!"

Tears unexpectedly welled in my eyes. "Not half as much as I care for you, you poisonous bitch!"

"Then I'll say it," she spat. "You're the dumbest ass I've ever met, 'cause you're killing yourself for something that's not even fucking real!"

I slapped her across the face as soon as the venomous words had left her mouth – *hard*. There was a deafening silence for a few seconds, but there was no time to fully digest what I'd done, as Petelia interrupted both of us with a piercing scream of her own.

"Soldiers!"

I turned my head and sure enough, there they were, not far off in the distance, moving like a cluster of tiny, evil ants, their distinctive black uniforms betraying their identity in seconds.

Queen Elsbeth's squadron.

Coming straight at us.

"You bastard!" I cried to the sorcerer who could no longer hear me. "You put us in their path on purpose!"

"Everybody run!" Petelia shouted.

Rebel, typically fast-acting, was already running like the wind, several meters ahead of Petelia and I. I quickly grabbed Petelia's hand and followed, though it really didn't matter which direction we went, because we couldn't run anywhere without being seen. We were on a wide-open desert plain with no trees or hills, in clear view for all to see and with nowhere to hide.

Our fates were sealed and we all knew it, but we still ran on blindly, as fast as our bodies would take us. I knew Rebel would never stop running and neither would I. Nor would Petelia. I wouldn't let her; I'd carry her over my shoulder and run till I dropped if I had to, as it was better to run and fight and be shot and killed for it, than to surrender to them and be screaming and begging for death later.

I prayed for a miracle. I prayed that fate would somehow spare me and the women I'd grown so fond of. I prayed that whatever the universe had in store for us, it wasn't the black cloud of punishment and torture that hovered so surely and so evilly. Please God, not that. Not us God, not that.

Then Elsbeth came to visit me again in my mind – and she burned fiercely inside, and in our moment of madness together,

I no longer feared my own death or thought about myself or the friends that had become so dear to me; I could only think of her.

I gritted my teeth.

Elsbeth, I thought, *no matter what happens, I'll never forget the promise I made. In this life or the next, I'll find you.*

Yes I will.

To be continued...

If you've enjoyed my novel, can you please leave a review? Thanks. Be sure to look out for my follow-up novel, 'The Darkness of Magic Book Two', where this story continues. Please keep checking my website <www.taniajoannepeterson.com> for exclusive news on when this book will be released.